AN

UNFORGETTABLE

MEMORY

A Love Mystery and Adventure

By
Colin Norman

AN UNFORGETTABLE MEMORY

Copyright @ 2021 Colin Norman

This novel is entirely a work of fiction. The names, characters and incidents portrayed in it are the work of the author's imagination. Any resemblance to actual persons, living or dead, events or localities is entirely coincidental.

Dedicated to my friends and family

Other Books by the Author

Fiction:

The Man Who Never Was: Love and Thriller, Mystery

A Near Miss From The Past: Thriller, Terrorist and Love Story

The Golden Adversity: Mystery, Thriller, Terrorists and Love story

An Unforgettable Memory: Mystery, Thriller, Adventure, Love story

NON Fiction:

Reach For The Stars: A story of transferring Social housing to a Housing Association

A Lifetimes Achievement: My Journey and story of over 47 years

AN UNFORGETTABLE MEMORY

Steve Long is in remission after having cancer treatment including radiation and a three-year monthly injection. He decides to have a week's holiday to help him recover and deal with his future.

On his break, by chance he meets a lady who is running away from her problem only for him to be drawn into it with his Investigation Firm, acting as a bodyguard to her.

This turns into a thriller, a love story with a mysterious kidnapping that's embroiled with many connections that MI5 are interested in.

The story is based in Norfolk with action in Nice, France and London, UK.

Steve is a friend of Mike and Jean who work for MI5; they have a strong interest in his case. He also has two colleagues, who work for him and are involved in the case. He is soon launched into an exciting adventure and was attracted to a lady that he met on his holiday. She plays a key part in luring him into the case.

The case moves at a fast pace and concludes with a thrilling twist, thus giving Steve a memorable experience, he will never forget!

Colin Norman

PART ONE
AN UNFORGETTABLE MEMORY
PROLOGUE

Steve had been ill for a while with cancer and had completed a treatment of tablets, injections, and radiotherapy. He had been told that apart from a low immune system and other side effects, the cancer was in remission and he needs to send to the Hospital's Oncology Department a blood sample every 6 months. They then inform him if his PSA level is within tolerance or not. It is at the moment although slowly getting higher and he does not have the strength he used to have and needs more sleep and rest. He also has many other underlying illnesses and takes a cocktail of tablets to keep him going.

Today he felt he would like to go away on holiday for at least 7 to 10 days, away from his usual but not so active life. He wanted to get some sun rays on him and to just relax on a beach with waves lapping the shore.He is single, divorced for many years and has three children, two boys and a girl, now with their own families, except his daughter who has no children. She lives about eight miles away and calls to see him regularly. He has nothing now to tie him down, nothing to stop him getting in his car and going away to his favourite coastal area in Norfolk.

So, he books a hotel near to Cromer, Norfolk. He starts to pack and rings his daughter to inform her of his holiday plans. She was delighted and said, "it will do you good dad, go and enjoy." So, he continued his packing, put fuel in the car and then went to bed to have a good night's rest.

He woke early in the morning at 6am, got everything sorted and then set off. As he was driving along the road; he thought to himself, I intend to enjoy myself or my name is not Steve Long. Little did he know, what lay ahead for him on this holiday!

AN UNFORGETTABLE MEMORY

Part 1

CHAPTER 1

The Start

Driving along, Steve felt totally carefree, all his troubles and woes were forgotten, the weather was blissfully sunny and there was very little wind.

He had decided to take an easy route to the coast so the journey would not be so long. Halfway through the journey, he took a break, turned off into a roadside café, parked the car and entered, the café wasn't very full. He ordered some toast and a hot pot of tea and sat down looking out of the window at all the different cars coming and going.

One car caught his attention as it came into the car park. It was a medium sized, grey coloured, Lexus. It parked near his car and out came a beautiful woman with long black hair, dressed in a short sleeve blouse, tight leggings, and some sort of what he thinks, are called sneakers, for shoes. As she got out, she stretched herself, put her bag on her shoulder and briskly walked into the café. She placed her meal order at the counter and then walked to sit at a table near Steve. His eyes followed her as she sat down. She looked at Steve, nodded and gave him a smile that could have enraptured any man's heart.

She then said, "isn't it a lovely day, are you travelling far?"

He smiled and replied, "Cromer."

"Oh" she replied surprised, "I'm going near Cromer, to Hotel Ashton."

Steve chuckled and said he was going there too!

She shook her head in amazement and giggled, "What a coincidence!"

"Yes" he remarked, "must be fate?" and she replied, "well, at least we will know each other."

Steve raised his eyebrows, smiled, and nodded "yes."

After a few minutes, Steve got up to leave and she said, "excuse me, I hope you don't consider it too forward of me, but if you are going to eat in at the hotel this evening, would you like to join me at my table?"

She then quickly followed it with "if you say yes, and I hope you do, then I shall arrange it."

Steve tried not to show his surprise and replied, "my name is Steve Long." And she said, "I'm Pat Morre."

Steve said, "I'm very pleased to meet you and I look forward to dining with you tonight. 7 pm, ok?"

He then said, "I must go", shook her hand and left to go the car park.

He then promptly set off once again on his journey. The road was getting slowly busy, so he decided not to take the Kings Lynne route and instead went more inland, which would take him directly to Cromer. Within 45 minutes, he was onto a one-way system through Cromer and then back out onto a coastal road. After a 15-minute drive, he turned off the main road and eventually arrived at the hotel's car park which led to a gravel driveway to a black and white building, surrounded by beautifully kept gardens of shrubs and flowers.

He checked in at reception, got his room key and made his way to a ground floor bedroom. He glanced round the room and then went to a window which looked across a medium sized lawn with a path around surrounded by a large variety of shrubs and plants most in full bloom with colourful flowers. A few trees were dotted around a shrubbery on the right and had a path leading through it. He smiled and thought, I wonder where that path leads to? He decided to find out and go exploring, the unpacking could be done later.

Steve took his shoulder bag which contained all his essential items and set off through the hotel reception's front doors. He saw a sign that indicated a path to the beach and as he walked down it, he smelt the fresh sea air, felt the warm sun, and took in several deep breaths, thinking, "I've made it, I didn't think 3 months ago, I would be able to do this. Great!"

The sand was warm, but he did not take his shoes off to walk on it. Instead he ambled down to the waves that were lapping on the shore and felt the wind. Although very gentle; blow the salt from the water over his lips and nose. It was invigorating.

He walked slowly along the seashore and eventually came to rocks and a cliff with waves breaking over the lower rocks and even the spray from this, energised him. He looked up to the top of the cliff and could see several people walking along it. One waved and so he waved back. He turned and walked back near to the bottom of the cliff in the shade and noticed a couple of families with children on the beach. As he came to the incline to go up, he found a rock to sit on; he took his shoes off to get the sand out. When he had finished, he turned and noticed a small area with sun loungers and brollies for hire with a waiter service from the hotel. He walked over and paid for an hour and then ordered a gin and tonic. He lay down on the sun bed, took his shirt off and opened a book that he had brought with him to read.

The gin and tonic soon came and Steve laid back sipping his drink and reading his book. After about half an hour he put the book down, got his binoculars out of his bag, sat up and scoured the beach and the sea. There were only a few boats out at sea, a small group of children playing in the sand near the cliffs in the shade and a couple walking along the sea edge in bare feet. He suddenly felt very tired so decided to go back to his hotel room for a nap.

CHAPTER 2

First Evening

He showered and changed into a formal shirt, grey slacks, a blazer, and no tie. He checked he had his money, bank cards, and door key card and then went to the bar in the dining room. It was about half full. He found a table and ordered a gin and tonic without lemon. He looked around and there was a mixed crowd, one group of about 12 people taking up 3 tables talking together. Steve was sipping his gin when a softly spoken female voice said, "may I join you?" He looked round and nearly fell over attempting to get up to offer her the other chair. She smiled, realising the effect she had on him. He casually said very calmly, "please do" and pulled out the chair and helped her take a seat. Pat chuckled and said, "thank you, kind sir. I see with you; chivalry is not dead!" He grinned and replied, "yes I try but usually end up knocking something over" and they both laughed loudly. She squeezed his hand and said, "What's that you're drinking?" he told her, and she asked for the same. Steve beckoned the waiter and ordered her a drink.

They walked into the dining room together and Steve noticed the glances they got from other diners. They sat at a table for two in the far corner of the room. Steve thought it was a good table to survey what was going on around them and he said, "Let's order our food and then we can get to know each other a bit." He looked around and commented, "I'm sure everyone thinks we are a married couple." She laughed and replied, "Are you bothered?" and saying this, she got the giggles, as did he. He replied that he didn't care what people thought, in fact he was happy for people to think they were a couple and said, "in fact, I should be so lucky......hey!!" He raised his glass of wine to her and she raised hers to touch his glass, both grinning at each other.

Steve then started the conversation by asking Pat if she was married as she was wearing a wedding band. She smiled at him and asked if he was? He replied, "Well I was, but now divorced." She commented, "I wear the ring to stop men pestering me." Steve looked at her and said, "I can imagine, some, maybe, but not all." She nodded, yes. So, he said, "well my story is I was married, have three children who are grown up and I do not see a lot of them. I've been single for a long while. Many years ago, I got a divorce and since then have not been inclined to marry again." Pat looked at him and said, "is this because you want to be single or for any other reason?" Steve was thinking of mentioning the cancer, but he decided to keep that to himself for now and instead replied, "no, never met the right one." Easy way out he thought. "Well" she said, "as we are being honest with each other, I have only been divorced about 6 months, my marriage was arranged by my father and my grandfather. I was young and used to having money and his family had money, so I went into it with both feet and ended up miserable, not having love and being someone who looked the part, wherever we went. I got fed up with it and got divorced but it was against my father's wishes."

She had tears in her eyes and Steve quickly said, "good for you, we only live once and so you should make the most of life and be with who you want to be with, live with, how you want to live and not the way that others want." She put her wine down and squeezed his hand, leaned over, and gave him a kiss. He looked at her as she got close to him and realised that she was older than he had first thought. He laughingly said, "I will have to think of something else nice to say, if I get that, every time." And they both giggled for a while.

They dropped talking about marriage when she said. "What are your plans for tomorrow?" He looked at her and replied. "Well to be honest, I haven't got a plan, just a whim. Always on my first day, I take a slow drive along the coast and see what I come across." She looked down as though she was embarrassed and slowly said, "Would you mind very much if I came with you?" then very quickly, she clarified that she did not know the area; she enjoyed his company and knew it would be enjoyable. Steve replied, "it would be my pleasure to show you around, I will be eating lunch somewhere, bring a bottle of water although I don't normally bother." He also mentioned that he would have breakfast at 9 am and be ready by 10.30 ish. He continued with "I know you will enjoy the day, Pat."

She smiled, stood up and took his arm to walk out the dining area. Steve said at the door, "would you like a walk around the garden before retiring?" She tossed her head and looked into his eyes saying, "Yes, that would be nice." So, they set off, arm in arm, down a path, then turned right and down the first junction of the path. They walked past lots of shrubs that were all in leaf and a few trees that took them to the cliff top. Steve could smell roses and a waft of sea air, these mixed together, made them both relax as they sat down on a bench facing the sea. Steve turned to Pat and remarked that now at last, he could feel his whole being relaxing and that her company was helping him do this. She replied, "well I must admit, I am relaxing too, being in your company."

They both sat there after saying this, gazing, out to the sea, watching a yacht in far horizon in full sail. Pat broke the silence by saying, "I'm so glad we are enjoying each other's company, and if you feel the same, then maybe we could spend time enjoying some more time together, tomorrow." She continued hurriedly stuttering, "Unless of course, you prefer to be on your own. I would understand?" He looked at her, shook his head and replied, "I cannot think of anything more enjoyable than spending our time together." She seemed pleased with that reply.

Steve said, "well tomorrow, I plan to drive along the coast and just stop and explore wherever takes my fancy." Pat quickly said, "That sounds great, I would like that, and I don't mind using my car!" He smiled and said, "ok, it's a date at 10.30 am as I go for breakfast at 9 am, so will be ready by this time." Pat said, "I think it's time for some rest now, so shall we head back to the hotel?" He nodded yes and stood up, turned, and helped her up; she took his hand saying, "Steve, you are a gentleman!" He just shrugged and said, "It's my pleasure marm," as she took his arm back to the hotel.

He accompanied her to her room door and said, "good night, Pat." She gave him her special smile, a quick peck on the cheek, said, "Good night, Steve" and then turned, opened her door, and went in. Steve walked away thinking that was a nice peck on the cheek. He was in very deep thought as he entered his room. He switched on the TV for low background noise and then sat on the bed thinking, how strange it had been to meet someone like Pat, who seemed to be happy in his company. He had no doubt that she was not short of money and was used to all the good things in life. He said to himself, "well now, let's just enjoy whatever we have together and stop being negative!" He was in bed soon after with these thoughts still on his mind.

CHAPTER 3

The First Day

Steve was up, showered, and ready to go to the dining room, at the time he had estimated he would do. He was seated by the waiter at the same table he had last night and before he could decide what he would have for breakfast, Pat's voice was in his ear, "morning, can I join you?" he turned and said, "of course, did you manage to have a nice sleep." She smiled and replied, "yes, I did, and I feel ready to enjoy our day." He smiled and replied, "Good that makes both of us." The waiter came and Steve ordered an English breakfast with toast and tea. So did Pat, to his amazement, as she was so slim!!

After breakfast, they went to their separate rooms to collect their bags to take with them for the day and both met up in the car park at Pat's car. They put the bags in the boot, wore their sunglasses and hats and set off with Steve instructing her on directions. The road was not very busy, and she went at about 40 mph enjoying the scenery on the way.

The sun was out and very warm. The air was fresh, and they had the side windows slightly open to let in the fresh sea air. Steve recognised she was a good driver and started to relax. After about half an hour's travelling, Steve spotted a beach sign and told her to turn at it. It was a gravel road with just enough room for cars to pass each other for a hundred meters or so and then opened into a rectangle with wire around which was obviously a parking area, so they parked there.

They both got out, Steve carried his binoculars and Pat took a small bag that had towels if required. They walked down a gradual slope of steps to the sand and shingle beach. It was not by most standard, a large beach but it already had several families with children playing and a few swimming in the sea, some building sandcastles, some just sitting and eating and others enjoying ice cream. Steve said to Pat, "I don't think we want to stay here too long; we need more facilities nearby and more space, I think." She looked at him held his hand and said, "I agree, but let's just sit a few minutes in the shade near the cliff and take in the sea air. He nodded yes and they both found a spot to sit down on near a rock for a back rest.

Pat pulled her hat down a little, she had her sun glasses on and looked at Steve saying, "Steve, I have not told you the whole story of why I am in this area and think I need to, as I am getting fond of you and you may not agree with why I am here." He sat with his hat on and sunglasses that hid his eyes and commented, "I better make myself more comfortable first before you start, so could you let me have a towel to sit on." Pat got the towels out and they both sat on one each. "Right" he said, "I'm listening."

"It is true, I have only been divorced for just over 6 months," she began saying, "but it took over a year of fighting my father, his father and my husband to get my decree nisi. I have no children and my life until now, has been ruled by those three men. The two fathers are very powerful and rich men in industry that includes property. My husband was chosen by them, to cement a business amalgamation of their core business on the property side.

I managed to get the majority shares in this business, and they did not realise that I am more than just a pretty face. It shook them up and they do not like it. I have been buying shares and together with the shares that they gave me when I had got married, I now have the controlling shares in the company.

They had thought that by arranging my marriage, my husband would attend all Board meetings instead of me and they could manipulate him to do whatever they needed for their benefit. However, he was more interested in his golf and spending money, than attending Board meetings. Everyone was ok until I became the majority shareholder and at the last AGM, I put forward ideas and restructures that other Board members accepted but not my two fathers or my husband. I was also made Chair of the Board. So, by divorcing my ex and becoming the Chair, it put them in a very difficult position, and they did have not the influence they needed, in order to do as they wished."

She stopped and looked at Steve with a worried look. He said, "it sounds as if you did the right thing, but why are you so worried and by the look on your face, so uptight and frightened?"

She said very tight lipped "they would not hesitate to get me out of the way. They are ruthless, powerful men and I have to have bodyguards even when I'm at home!!"

Steve took his glasses off and said, "No wonder you are frightened and tried to get away incognito." Taking off her glasses, she replied, "Does this make you want to stop seeing me? As I have no doubt, they have people looking for me at this moment."

Steve looked at her, the sun making him squint and said, "I am partnering you because we gel and get on so well together and I think we can have a nice holiday together! Being the person I am, having spent a lot of my life in investigation as a private company, I do not like anyone, rich or poor, to be bullied and by all means, it does sound like you are being harassed by your Father and Father in law. That needs to be sorted. Also, you are entitled to live your life as you wish it to be, not how they want it to be just to feed their avarice. Your problem is, you will not know who the good guys are from bad, especially if they find out where you are." Pat shuddered and replied, "to right, I will not, so I'm hoping they will not find me! But

Steve, I am grateful you still wish to be my friend, thank you."

He then sat a minute thinking and looked at her and said, "I have friends who I can contact and who owe me a favour and provided they have the time, they could help in many ways." She smiled and said, "Would you?"

He nodded yes and retorted, "so for now, let's get on with enjoying our day." They walked up the incline to the car park and set off again along the coast road. After about 20 minutes, Steve said "turn left at the next junction and go about 40 meters to a small café, called Sea Shore Café and park."

Pat did this and they then went to the café. It was a well looked after establishment that he had visited before and found the service and cooking very nice, plus it had a reasonable selection of drinks, including alcohol, if required. They sat at a table near the window and a waitress in a spotless pinafore came up, she recognised Steve and said, "Do you want the usual?" He grinned at her saying, "yes tea, BLT sandwiches" and then turned to Pat who quickly said, "Same for me please."

They looked at each other, Pat smiled and said, "I

am enjoying this" and Steve smiled back with a "me too" reply.

The sandwiches came and Steve gently said to Pat, "if I contact my friends who are MI5 agents, they will investigate everything. Are you happy with this?" She replied, "I've not got anything to hide, they may have but that's their problem, not mine".

He nodded his head and changed the subject to talking about the next part of the journey. He said that he could remember that nearby there were quite a few caravan and chalet sites with some decent facilities. There was one that he wanted to look at as he had a nice holiday there and it would be interesting to see if it had altered. Pat replied, "Sounds great, look forward to it." Then she asked him if he would like to drive and he agreed. So, they finished their meal, left the café and started on the next part of their journey. The roads were getting a lot busier and they were only able to do a steady speed in the traffic. After about twenty minutes, he took a left turn into an entrance and drove down a metalled road to a chalet park. It had a lot of brick built and portable chalets, all set out very nicely, giving each one its own little plot and privacy. Nearby to the big car park, were several shops and a café. He drove down to the car park and chose a space under some trees to shade the car. Pat said, "this looks nice, particularly for children."

Steve said, "yes, and by the number of cars in this car park there are not many visitors today!"

He turned to Pat and said, "do you want to look at the beach first and then maybe decide if you want to stay or move on?" She nodded a yes, so they picked up their bags and as they walked down the steps to the beach, Pat pointed to a small cluster of sun beds and brollies, "what about relaxing on those for a while and just enjoy the beach and water?" He replied that it sounded like a good idea and no point in rushing everywhere. They both went over, and Steve paid a man so they could slump down on sun beds with their sunglasses and hats on. Pat had discarded her shirt and was getting the rays lying down. Steve got out his binoculars, took his sunglasses off and slowly surveyed the beach and then turned to seaward. He could about just see in the distance a ship which looked like a tanker with its shape. He scanned further right of this and spotted a small sailing boat coming into shore. Further to the right, there were children and adults playing in the sea. He followed the waves to the shore and saw children and dads building sandcastles, of sorts. A normal scene near the sea in Norfolk. The sun was shining; he lay back on the sun bed, just thinking.

His thoughts went to what had happened since his coming to the coast - the meeting with Pat, her unhappy marriage, her rise to the Chair of the Board of her Fathers and Father in law's business, her concern about being harmed because of this, surely, they would not need to do her any harm, unless they thought she knew something that she could use against them.

His train of thought was broken by Pat saying, "I think I've had enough sun at the moment," sitting up and putting her shirt on. Steve replied, "Ok, let's go back to the car and head off to somewhere else." He smiled at her, helped her up and they went back to the car park and set off on the journey.

CHAPTER 4

The Mystery

It was a sunny, cloudless sky, 10 am on a Saturday morning and three males were in deep conversation in an office in a large company in London. Voices were raised sometimes and all in certain speeches, gesticulating to make their individual points. A tall man, who was speaking, had a deep voice, a voice that sounded like he was used to being in control and being obeyed. He was Peter Morre, a high-powered, wealthy businessman, who often got his own way. He was well-dressed, 60 years old with grey hair at the sides, but in a way that certain women thought was very attractive. He was pointing his finger at a man sitting opposite him and said, "We cannot let this situation carry on, it is bad for our image and not what we had planned for the amalgamation."

The man he was speaking to was very Latin looking with straight black, greying hair. He was Josh Rodriguez, who had immigrated to England in the 50s, making his fortune in property. He too was in an expensive, tailored suit. He was about 6-foot-tall, wore glasses and cut a fine figure, despite being 65 years old. He looked at Peter, smiled a crooked smile and replied very sternly, "it's not the first thing that has altered since our amalgamation and affected our image, but we got over it!" and continued "what about the CEO you appointed while I was on holiday abroad?" Peter's face went bright red with fury and he was about to shout back when the third man interjected, "let's not get into a squabble, we are here to sort this problem out, no matter how it has happened." He was Joe Morre, Peter's son, and ex-husband of the now new chair, Pat Morre. He continued, "look we know that it affects us all, especially now that Pat has taken over, being the majority shareholder and she has the backing of most of the board. Plus, the CEO supports her ideas of restructure. If it makes the company more efficient, then what's the problem?"

Peter and Josh looked at each other and grimaced. Peter replied, "the problem is that she has control of our large empire that we worked our hands to the bone to make a success of and we arranged your marriage so that the company could stay in the family, so that no one can or ever will have control over us." Josh said, "I must admit she has grasped the business well and exceeded much more than I expected from her" and then directing his look at

Joe, he continued "your philandering didn't help and cost us quite a bit to sort out."

Joe grimaced and looked down at the floor saying, "I admit that caused the divorce, but Pat did not suddenly acquire shares and come up with a restructure in the time that it took her to. It didn't just happen because of my unfaithfulness; she must have studied and worked out a plan to take over at least a year ago!" Peter interjected with, "and she knows it would neutralize our control over her life and marriage! Josh, she is a chip of the old block." Joe said, "Well none of this is getting us anywhere and unless we remove her as Chair, she has the upper hand!!"

They all looked at each other and Josh broke the silence "we could frighten her, but I don't want any harm to come to her!" The other two looked at each other and one at a time, slowly agreed.

Peter said, "I have in my employ, one or two people who could do this job very efficiently but we must get our plans on the merger we planned for moving and sorted, so it's imperative we sort this quickly." Joe agreed and added "as long as you remember what I have just said.". They then stood up and Josh left. Peter and Joe left together and drove a few miles to one of Peter's other offices.

In the office, Peter sat behind the desk, picked up the

phone and said, "Mack have you got a minute, can you come to my office."

Mack came and sat down beside Joe. Peter explained the problem with Pat and that he wanted him to let her know the danger she could put herself in, if she continued being the Chair and the main shareholder. He told Mack to frighten her but not to harm her. He said, "she has bodyguards. I think she is in England, on the east coast having a break but she has not taken the bodyguards."

Joe said. "Find her and discreetly remind her who she is and what she should do to relinquish some shares at a good price, to make everyone happy."

Mack looked at both of them with a smirk on his face and said, "I will be the perfect gent but she will have no doubt she will have to do what you have indicated, but I must have your acceptance that if she does not do so, then she pays the consequence!!" He sat and waited for an answer and it was Peter who replied that it would only be the very last resort and an accident. "You contact me before you take that course! Understood?" and Mack replied, "perfectly."

Steve and Pat had turned a few miles inland and were doing a circle which would take them back to Cromer and to their hotel. The road was not very busy and as they drove, Steve noticed a sign advertising a well-known house open to visitors. He told Pat to turn left if she wanted to look at an ancient house that she might find interesting and there was also a café. She smiled, agreed, said ok and turned at the next junction. She continued for about a mile down the road, followed the signs to a car park, paid and then they walked to a large entrance to the courtyard of the building. Steve pointed to the far corner to a sign indicating the café. On the way to the cafe, Pat said, "Steve I'm really enjoying a freedom I've never experienced before!" He smiled and said, "Stick with me; you will see things you would never experience in your other life, Pat!"

After their cuppa, they took a stroll around the house with its many small stalls and large rooms selling various articles, some antique and others more like items found at car boot sales. They enjoyed this and strolled around, laughing and joking like a pair of teenagers.

Steve looked at his watch, it was 4 pm, so he suggested they head back to the hotel as he had a few calls to make and they could also decide on dinner tonight. The walked back to the car and as they got very close to where they had parked, a female suddenly came up very quickly to Pat, showed her a press card and asked, "aren't you

Pat Morre, the Chair of the R&M group organisation?" Pat stopped and looking at Steve, she was taken aback. Steve said to the reporter, "I know you have a job to do, but we do not want any publicity or problems, so please no pictures or statements, it's just an old fashioned holiday break, but if you give me your card, I can arrange for one another time. However, if you don't mind a Pat Morre look alike!!... And, they are also willing to pay for it? The reporter looked very crest fallen and said, "She certainly looks like her?" Steve said, "Well that's how we earn the money!" "Oh" she said, "I apologise, here's my card," and left them. Steve said to Pat, "That's put the cat among the pigeons."

They got into the car and Steve drove and at same time, kept an eye out to see if they were being followed.

By the time they got near Cromer and turned onto the coast road, Steve was satisfied that they had not been followed. He said to Pat, "Tonight, we must discuss whether to stay in this area or move on. If the reporter is as good as I think she might be, she will try and trace where we stay and follow us." Pat had now recovered to her usual calm self and replied, "I think so too."

Steve was sure the reporter had not followed them, so he drove directly to the hotel and parked. They went into the reception and as they walked by the desk, the receptionist said to Pat, "I had a phone call enquiring if you were staying here, but of course, I said I could not say yes or no, as we do not give out information on any of our guests, without their permission."

Pat said, "thank you, did they give a name?" The receptionist shook her head saying, no.

Steve listened to this and put his hand on the elbow of her right arm and walked with her to her room, saying on the way, "Can I come in and have a quick chat please?" Pat said "yes."

In the room, Pat asked if he would like a drink and commented, "Can I share my small whisky with you?" Steve nodded, yes.

Pat got the bottle out of the fridge and poured it into two mugs saying, "Sorry I do not have any glasses." Steve lifted his mug to toast her and said in his best Humphrey Bogart voice, "here's looking at you kid." They both giggled.

He then said, "well, thinking on what you explained to me about your family finding you and the pressure that they would put on you if they do, it is unfortunate that they have found out that you are in this area."

Pat scowled and replied, "yes they will very quickly be on the lookout for me and will search this area to find me!"

Steve smiled and said "this brings our friendship into a different position.

I will try and protect and partner you wherever you want to go, but I need help and I will have to contact and use my business resources to do so.

This being the case, may I ask, do you wish to employ my firm for this, or do you have any others that you would rather use?" Pat looked at Steve, took his hand and said, "I want you to do this please, because I'm enjoying your company and I trust you."

He replied, "in that case can you give me time to make a couple of phone calls. I will come back to you on this at dinner tonight in the restaurant."

She smiled and nodded yes. Steve stood up, left and went to his room.

Steve sat pondering on Pat's situation for ten minutes. He then picked up his mobile phone, rang Mike who worked at MI5, and who was a friend of his from the days they served in the Marine commandos. It was answered by Mike's wife, Jean, mother to their 9-year-old daughter. She told him that Mike was out, back about 6 pm and asked if she could help? Steve told her the whole story about his holiday, meeting Pat Morre and the position she was in. He asked if they could investigate the R&M group, due to the meeting of the reporter and his concern on what may happen to Pat. They both passed the usual pleasantries and then he rang off.

Steve then rang his own firm. His call was answered by an employee called Tony, who did most of the protection and investigation work provided by Steve. Tony said, "Hi Steve, how's your break going?" Steve informed him of all that had happened and how the firm now had the job of protecting Pat and finding out what the two fathers and ex-husband's intentions were. He then said, "I want you and Diane to find out as much as you can about the group." Tony was eager to do this and Steve had no doubt he would enjoy a chance to make enquires about them, plus he would be handy if things got physical. Steve was aware he was an ex-commando and boxing champ in the forces. He certainly looked like a boxer and kept himself in good shape.

His other employee was Diane, an attractive, ex-forces as well and able to look after herself, if needed to. They made a good team. Steve finished with, "get Diane to make enquiries about Pat and any friends and companions, male and female, please. Let me know what you find out as I'm going to be her constant companion while she is here. Book it down to charge Pat Morre."

He was just finishing when Diane came on the

phone and said in her usual, sensible manner, "Steve you are still a long way getting better with your cancer, etc. so be careful and don't overdo it." He replied "yes marm" and cut off. Steve then set about getting ready for his evening meal with Pat.

CHAPTER 5

The Case Begins

Pat had just got to the door to go down for dinner when her phone rang. A male voice came on, she recognised it as *Mack,* a henchman and bodyguard

of Peter Morre, her father in law. She answered "yes", and he said *Mr Joe Morre and Peter send their regards. They have asked me to contact you to explain that you have put yourself in a position of dividing the R&M business into three sides, when at the moment they have an amalgamation being discussed. It is not very agreeable to them and wants me to ask ...*" he paused a few seconds, waiting for a reply. Pat stayed silent so he continued, "*if you will accept selling some of your shares to even this up. You will be offered more than they are worth, and you will also remain Chair of the business.*"

Pat took a deep breath and replied, "One, Mack, I do not do this type of business second hand, they can face me themselves. Two, I am on a break and how did you know I was here? And three, you all know how hard I have worked to get to this position so you all can forget it, until I discuss this matter with the Board." She put the phone down and sat down on the bed shaking with trepidation and a little anger. She then pulled herself together, tided herself in the mirror and left the room.

Steve was in the bar area waiting and as she came up to him, he stood and said "it's a little crowded here, shall we get a table in the dining room? I've already asked for a table on its own in a corner where we can talk freely."

She nodded and as they walked in, a waiter came up to them and said he had booked a nice quiet table over in the right-hand corner.

They sat down, ordered wine and their usual meal. The wine came and Steve poured a glass each and said to Pat, "You look very beautiful, except for the worried frown you have got." He touched her glass and said, "To our holiday" and smiled. She forced a smile back, he recognised this and so, he said, "well, what has happened?" She smiled realising how observant he was and replied, "I have had a phone call from a henchman of my father in law." She gave him a rundown of the main facts of the conversation.

Steve leaned back in his chair and asked, "Which phone did he contact you on? Mobile or the land line?" Pat said, "My mobile."

Steve looked at her smiling and commented, "so they don't know where you are yet! Good. So, relax he is not going to turn up yet!" She smiled and said to him, "Steve I needed that saying to calm me down, thank you."

He took her hand and patted it saying, "I will now tell you what I have arranged to do." Whilst he was enjoying the steak he had ordered, he told her who he had contacted and spoken to. As he was finishing his main course, he said to her, "I think the best plan is to carry on as we have done so far and stay in this area. My people will keep an eye on our backs and their contacts will produce a certain amount of information for us to consider. Simply put we do not let them spoil our break to-gether; we will take things how and as they come! I will get my people to come now and stay here and they will act as friends we have met up with. Also, my friend at MI5 is looking into all this and they will come back to me as soon as they have any information." They finished their meals and Pat said, "can we go for a walk again to clear my mind?" "Certainly," replied Steve.

They left the dining room, walked past reception and onto the garden path, turned right down it to the seat on the cliff top. Pat remarked, "I know this is a simple walk along the cliff top, but I feel so relaxed when we walk it, even though I know that next week is not going to be easy." Steve looked at her smiling and replied, "That's the point of a short break from work, it recharges your batteries. Enjoy these pleasures while you can, I need this myself to help me get back my energy and strength after work."

As he said this a breeze had started and the sea air and scented flowers drifted over them and they both sat there relaxed and free of the daily troubles for a minute or two. A few seagulls flew over squawking away. The sound of waves hitting the rocks came in spasms of sound. A very faint sound of music in the distance mixed with the rustle of the leaves in the bushes and trees. They both just sat and felt at peace with the world.

Pat took his hand and said, "Steve, I am so lucky and grateful that I have met you here, but the next week or so could be hectic and very troublesome to the extreme." He laughed replying, "I hope so, otherwise I would get bored and restless as my occupation is dealing with your type of problem." "I know" she said looking serious, "but I think looking at you, you did come here for some recuperation, not to work!"

He looked at her with a frown on his brow and said, "But it's my way of recuperating, so don't worry." Thinking to himself, he felt tired and needed to get some rest. So, he stood up and helped her up saying, "let's get back to our rooms and get some rest then, shall we?" Pat nodded yes and stood up. On the way back to the hotel Steve asked her to let him know if she received any calls or contact, he also mentioned that he would order a local newspaper for tomorrow. They parted at her room door saying good night.

In his room, he rang Tony and asked if he had any updates? Tony very quickly gave Steve a rundown of having found out the share situation at R&M, Pat's divorce settlements and that he would be arriving at the hotel in the morning. Steve was pleased and replied, "Good, I will think about how we can arrange your cover and on how to introduce you. Put all you have found out in an email to me and please ask Diane to do the same. Are you both coming together?" "No" he said, "in separate cars." "Ok then" Steve said and cut off.

He then checked his emails to see if Mike or Jean

had sent anything. They had not!! He decided to leave everything and go to bed; he felt very exhausted and would sort it all out in the morning.

Steve was woken by his mobile ringing at 7.30 am. It was Mike, his mate in MI5. Steve picked it up, murmured "hello" and Mike said, "Sorry Steve if I woke you but I have a busy day in front of me." "I thought" he continued, "I should inform you before you get in too deep with the R&M group that we are doing an investigation of them as they are trying to amalgamate with a firm that has a lot of MOD Contracts. This is normal procedure, but we have heard one or two things about share trading and bully boy tactics from the Morre's father and son." Steve replied, "Thanks Mike, this is why I wanted you to look into them. It looks like I will need to watch my back too so thanks for the warning." "Ok" replied Mike, "speak later" and rang off.

Steve felt tired and lacked energy; he knew his illness was the cause.

He thought the Morre's and to some extent, Rodriguez, dominated everything and how it would stick in their throat if they were to lose all their control to Pat thus reducing their dominance, but then again, this was nothing that was worth harming her for. Also, given that if the other firm amalgamated with them, then their share issue would alter anyway! No, Steve thought, there had to be something else. He and his people would have to find out what this was all about.

He went down the corridor and, on the way; he knocked on Pat's door, saying "It's me, Steve! I'm going for breakfast." Pat replied, "Ok, see you down there!" He smiled to himself and went to the dining room. Within a few minutes, Pat joined him, and they ordered an English breakfast with toast. Steve told her that she looked very nice. He liked the cotton top, slacks and canvas shoes she was wearing. She certainly did not look her age.

Pat replied, "Well you look tired Steve, bad night? Hope you are not overdoing it? Not used to the dashing about" Steve smiled and replied, "no, just a lot going through my mind. I think we should, if you agree, spend the day here, on the beach and in the hotel. I have two colleagues arriving and they will watch us 24/7." He also mentioned that they could spend some time to plan what was left of their stay and discuss some questions he had about her Father, Father in law and ex-husband.

Pat smiled and said, "I have no problem with that. I can get my hair done and I will answer everything you wish to know." She raised her eyebrows to make Steve believe she was an innocent person! Steve laughed and said, "Well try and book a hair appointment for10 am as my people will be here by then and we will iron out the creases in our plan. You will be discreetly observed at all times."

As they were walking back to their rooms, Steve took a call on his phone and when he finished, he said to Pat, "my two colleagues have arrived, shall we go and meet them in reception?" She nodded a yes and so they made their way there. Tony and Diane were stood talking to each other near a group of chairs. Tony noticed Steve with an attractive lady who had black hair, walking towards them. His face had a wide smile and he said, "Well fancy meeting you two here?"

Steve shook his hand and introduced Pat and they all sat down, talking to each other like people who had not met up for years. Steve invited them for lunch in the bar area which had a section outside with tables provided under a canopy. He also explained that they could meet in his room for a briefing as Pat had to go to the hairdresser. So, they all parted and went to their rooms. Steve then took Pat to the hair saloon and walked back to his room to meet Tony and Diane.

Diane provided a quick update and then went to the hairdressers to keep an eye on Pat and she was to inform him when she was finished. This she did, not having any replies yet to her enquiries about Pat through her channels of information. After this, she left.

Tony had found out that there was no close friendship between Josh and Joe and the only way, Josh had agreed to the amalgamation was by giving shares to Pat, his daughter, not realising that when she married Joe's son, that it gave the Morre's a chance to control, pushing Josh out on many occasions. Except in the acquisition of other companies which is when he normally got Pat to support him.

Steve smiled and replied, "I assume this agreement was before she married Joe's son?" Tony nodded a yes, grinning and then saying, "Many a slip, etc."

Steve said, "Ok this gives them a reason for trying to get Pat's shares, but not to the extent of harming her!!" Tony agreed, it was no reason to harm her and surely, they shall have to renegotiate the shareholding, etc. However, they decided to continue to protect Pat on the assumption that there was a risk of her being threatened and psychologically, intimidated!

Steve said, he would leave Diane and Tony to make that sure that Pat was adequately covered on the protection side and get other known people to help who have worked with their firm before. He then suggested they all have dinner at the hotel tonight and thereafter, only meet up when it was considered necessary. Steve said, "Cheerio" and that he would see them later.

Mack had reported back to Peter Morre senior about Pat's comments and had been told to put careful pressure on her but not to contact her personally, face to face, until they had asked him to. "Um" he thought, "I best stick to phone calls, text and email then at the moment." In the meantime, he would get his own peoples support to find out where she was holidaying?

Peter had informed Josh and Joe about his order to Mack and that he wanted to meet them in the office tomorrow at 11am. He then phoned a private detective that he had contracted to follow Pat and report directly to him only. This detective was called Frank and he replied, "Will do, is it urgent?" "Yes, it is" replied Peter and Frank said "I will get straight on it.

Steve met Pat coming out of the hairdressers and

suggested they go back to her room for a chat.

CHAPTER 6

The Enigma

The mist was just lifting as Peter Morre was being chauffeured to his office in London. He sat very pensive, opened his newspaper but could not concentrate. He was not in a good mood for meeting the others, but as always, when he was in this mood, he puffed on a Havana cigar. He had decided in his mind that Pat needed a shock to make her come to her senses and to consider the merger their way. The car turned into the ten floor buildings underground car park and parked in his reserved bay. The chauffer opened his door and Peter got out, took the lift to the 9th floor, before transferring to another guarded lift to the 10th floor. This was only for the owners of the company and Board members.

Peter was the first to arrive, so he sat down and went through his letters and emails. One was from the owner of the company who was negotiating terms of an amalgamation with; it was requesting a meeting for next Friday, 10.30 am.

He wrote 'ok arrange' on the note and put it in the tray for his secretary's attention. Josh Rodriguez then knocked on his door came in and sat facing him. "Morning, Peter have you read the note for the amalgamation meeting? It's ok with me?" Peter nodded yes and then with a frown, he said, "Pat's not cooperating then?" Josh looked at him and frowning, he replied "surely you did not expect her to, she is, don't forget a chip of the old block - me!"

Peter grinned and retorted, "Yes obstinate" Josh replied "and does not budge easily. Warnings and threats will not make her change her mind, so I suggest a very good business plan for her to read and lull her into an agreement. Forget about your bully boy tactics and do what we should have done first. In the meantime, we go forward as we are doing and get the agreements for the new subsidiary."

Peter sat back and said, "yes I think that would be the best way, but we have to get the result we want from it. Let's give that a try and use the people who normally negotiate for us before we do the nitty-gritty. I will set that in motion." Josh stood up and replied, "Good, keep in touch but remember, I don't want any harm to come to her!!" He then left.

Peter pressed his intercom, a female voice answered, and he asked her to contact a firm he had always used in these matters.

He then sat pondering on what Josh had said and

after some deliberation; he picked the phone up and rang his son. Joe answered and Peter gave him a run-down of his conversation with Josh. He then asked "Joe, do you think you could talk to her and explain the reason we need to get some shares from her to level up the playing field in the negotiation for amalgamating the company that operates on contracts for the MOD." Joe went silent for a moment and then replied, "Yes I can have a word and try to convince her that it is in the interest of the company, but I know from experience, if she puts a wall up, she can be very stubborn. However, I will try in the next few days and come back to you." Peter sat puffing away at his cigar, deep in thought.

The firm that Peter had rang was Price & Co., a very experienced and successful negotiating firm that specialised mainly in being able to get a deal when it seemed impossible to get one. Their top man was Alan Price, who had started the business and now, could pick and choose his work but the R&H Group were a lucrative company and so he was eager for the contract. He told his PA to collate all the information they had asked for and he would also make some enquiries through his own contacts.

Pat and Steve were discussing the problem from Pat's point of view in her room. Steve explained how he had organised protection for her using

Tony and Diane as her father and father in law would be now be trying to find out where she was staying on her holiday. They would then probably arrange for someone to meet her in person to either frighten her into selling shares or to persuade her that it would be in her best interests to do so. This is precisely where Steve and his people would come in and he advised her, that at no time should she negotiate or meet anyone on her own.

He then continued to talk about her holiday at the hotel. His opinion was that she should stay and carry on as they had done so far, as she would be with him most of the time with back up from his team. If anyone approached her, he would deal with it. He explained that if she did not then she risked the danger of being kidnapped! Steve said to her, "I'm afraid it will mean that I shall be keeping very close to you and I hope you will not mind that?" She looked at Steve, swung her hair over her shoulder and coyly giggled, "Well at least that gives me something to look forward to."

Steve continued, "the other point that crossed my mind is that you should consider using an expert shares negotiation firm to act in your best interests to negotiate and deal with any requests to buy your shares. All requests will have to go through them, and they will then follow your instructions." He further explained that whilst this might lessen some of the pressure put on her, it would not take away the danger and harm that she could be threatened with. Pat looked at him and said "Steve! I knew I would get bullying and threats, but I am still Josh's daughter and I know he would never harm me! Even so, I'm glad to have your company looking after that side of things." Steve smiled at her and nodded yes. He then changed the subject and said, "Let's go have some lunch then spend time on the beach this afternoon. Try and enjoy our holiday."

After lunch, they both walked down to the beach and chose an umbrella with sun beds that were partly in the shade. Steve sat on one and put his bag near it and then asked Pat if she was going to catch some rays for a while. She moved her bed from under the umbrella and took off her clothes to reveal a bikini and a marvellous figure; she also noticed the admiring look she got from Steve. With a sun hat and glasses on, she lay down catching the sun's rays, apparently feeling very content.

Steve sat there and having got his binoculars out was looking through them out to sea, but his mind was going over his present responsibility for looking after Pat. He wondered about telling her about his cancer and he thought now was the right time to tell her. Suddenly he was jolted back to the present by his mobile phone ringing, it was Mike!

"Hello Mike" Steve said, "any news?" Mike replied, "well yes, I have got news. First, I have had a talk to 'T' who wants you to keep in touch and will give you help if needed! MI5 are investigating the running of the group and trying to find anything that may need our attention. Also, it will have to go to the CMA (Competition and Markets Authority) commonly called the Competition Ombudsman, before the merger can happen. To be honest, we have heard one or two shady deals attributed but not proven to be connected to Peter and Joe Morre! Peter is a dangerous man, so Steve watch your back."

Steve smiling replied, "What another one to watch?" Then giggling said, "I will, and my team are with me, but I'm puzzled why they are so riled up and making it such a big deal. I think there is more to this than just the merger!!" "Me too" said Mike, "take care, keep in touch." Steve put the phone back in his pocket and sat thinking.

Pat sat up and said, "Would you like a drink?"

her hands shading the sun from her eyes. He nodded yes and she beckoned a waiter as he was going by and asked him to bring two G +Ts. He bowed and smiling said "yes, Miss Morre." Pat turned to Steve and commented, "You look deep in thought. Problems?" He laughed saying, "sorry, just thinking and planning." Pat looked at him with a puzzled look on her face replying, "Are you sleeping ok? You look really tired!!" Steve looked at her with a serious face and said, "Pat, we have got fond of each other and learned to trust each other, so I think it's time I put you in the picture about myself. A year ago, I was diagnosed with cancer. I have had the treatment and radiation therapy but finished on injections every three months. It has made me lose weight and feel very weak. I also have many side effects from the treatment and a low immune system. At the moment I'm winning but I do get tired. As for my business, I have a good team and I have good people who work for me like the two, who you have met."

He looked into her eyes and there were tears in them. She found a hanky and dabbed them saying, "thanks for telling me Steve, it does not alter anything. I know you will do your job." He sat down beside her, put his arm on her shoulder squeezing, "yes, I like that" then more gently saying, "I do not want sympathy, but understanding.

I may sometimes need to rest; otherwise I carry on as normal and will be the same person. I admit I cannot guarantee a long-term friendship but let's be honest in this day and age, who can!!"

She kissed him saying "Steve let's enjoy what time we get, the best we can." Steve replied, "yes, I would like that, although it does not make me feel romantic, as much as I used to!" She giggled, smiling at him; "it's your company I like and look forward to."

By this time their drinks had come. Pat signed for them and they sat side by side, just enjoying each other's company and smiling. Steve then said, "I don't think we should let your in-laws ruin this week, we should carry on and forget about them." She put her head on his shoulder and said, "yes, I agree."

And then, "Steve, I think I have done enough sunbathing for now, can we head back to the hotel?" Steve nodded yes, so they got their things together and walked back up the slope to the hotel. Neither of them had noticed Diane get up off a sunbed further along and follow them at a distance back to the hotel. She got to the front door and entered and was joined by Tony and they both sat discreetly watching Steve and Pat who were now walking through to the conservatory adjoining the dining room area.

Diane said to Tony very carefully "I think the two of them are gelling together, do you think he has mentioned his illness to her?" Tony replied looking thoughtful and commented, "Knowing Steve, I would say yes!!"

She smiled and said, "I hope so too, they go so well together, it would be nice to see Steve happy again!" Tony nodded yes and stood up and watched as they went into the conservatory for lunch. The rest of the afternoon Steve and Pat just enjoyed themselves walking around the gardens, also sitting holding hands on the seat on the cliff top. The evening was spent enjoying a meal in the dining room and some time talking in Pat's room before they retired. Neither of them was aware of either Tony or Diane in the background.

Peter Morre received a phone call while visiting one of their firm's subsidiaries. It was Alan Price, of Price & Co, a share dealer informing him that he had been contacted by Marcus & Co representing Pat Morre. He was told that anything to do with her shares or interests had to be negotiated through them and no one else. Alan said, "I assume you expected this and asked everything to go through him personably and he will report back only to Joe?" Peter grunted and said, "Yes, only through him. I leave it with you Alan. Keep in touch!"

Peter sat back in his chair and contemplated his next move on the shares. Does he still put pressure on Pat to sell? Would it be wiser to leave it at the moment, as knowing Pat, she does not take to being pressured very kindly! On this subject, no, he thought leave it as she is expecting it to be between the two share dealers only for a short time. This will see how she thinks, then decide on the next step. After all, with the monopoly people about, they must not find out about this part of the proposed merger. He sent emails to Josh and Joe to this effect and to his Hench man, Mack, informing him to cool it, until further notice. He stood up, walked to the window, and considered his next move! A smile came on his face as he watched a squirrel run up a tree with its hoard of nuts. Yes, winters quickly coming this year.

Steve and Pat continued their holiday, exploring the coast; they even went to a bird sanctuary and a trip to the Cromer Pavilion Theatre to enjoy a show. They walked along the cliff tops and enjoyed the sea air and sun, just having a normal holiday break. The days went by quickly and it was a relief to Steve that nothing had happened to spoil their holiday as they had both enjoyed each other's company.

On the last night when they had their evening meal Steve broached the future. He told Pat he would move close to her house near London and if she agreed, he would act as her escort on any event she needed an escort for.

Her present staff could cover everything else, including her home. He had contacted them and arranged all this. She smiled, said she would be very happy with the arrangement, "I have really enjoyed this holiday especially your company but I will on my return home, put on my business head and be the business woman about town" - she gave Steve a big smile. He looked at her and said, "I would expect nothing different" and smirked.

They then returned to their rooms, he said goodbye and that he would see her in London. She put her arms around his neck, gave him a very passionate kiss, turned and not looking back and went into her room. Steve went to his room, with mixed feelings churning in his stomach.

CHAPTER 7

The Mystery

The morning came, Pat had left early, and he was joined at breakfast by Tony, who brought him up to date on what they had now accumulated together, information on this job from his contacts. Tony said "Steve, did you know Pat has a twin sister who left her father 4 years ago and he has stripped her of anything to do with his wealth and home. Josh Morre does not admit she is his daughter and thinks she is involved with ruthless people. He will not have her name mentioned in his presence."

Steve looked at Tony shocked, as he never dreamt of this being part of the puzzle. Tony continued "we are investigating where she is and who she is with at the moment!" Tony then mentioned Pat's father in law saying, "Peter Morre is a man to be very wary off. It is rumoured he has mafia connections in America and Italy and is known to be a ruthless man."

Steve said, "I am getting him checked out by my mate Mike at MI5 and I will give him all the info we have. Can you put that in an email to me?"

"Ok" said Tony. Steve continued, "Keep up your enquiries on the daughter. I am not happy until we know the whole situation and I have a niggle in my mind there is more going on, far more than Pat knows, somewhere in this mystery. Why is it so important to get some of Pat's shares? Is there more going on in the company than we can all see? There is an underlying mystery somewhere hidden from us. I can feel it in my bones."

Tony laughed and said, "one of your gut feelings again, Steve? I will do as you say," They both grinned and went their separate ways from the dining room.

Peter was sitting in his dining room enjoying his breakfast and was tucking into his poached egg, bacon, tomatoes with toast when his butler came in and said to him, "Mack is here to see you sir." Peter looked at him and replied "send him in and please set another place. "Mack walked in and Peter still eating said, "Help your self Mack, there is plenty." Mack went over to the food and started lifting the lids of the containers and piling his plate. The butler returned and put a cup and saucer and a pot of coffee on the table and positioned a chair opposite Peter. Mack with a full plate walked to the seat and started to eat. In between a bite of bacon, Peter without looking at him said, "Well what is on your mind?" Mack stopped eating a minute and said, "I've had an idea on the Pat Morre problem, and I need to talk it over with you. It is something we could be doing while everything is being negotiated elsewhere!" Peter now drinking his tea said, "so what is it then?" Mack replied, "First, it will not interfere with the negotiations and would be a safeguard whatever happens." Peter stopped eating and said, "So what is it?" Mack with a big grin on his face said, "I've found Josh's other daughter, the twin, and I have at this moment someone with her, who is getting to know her. No one would be able to tell the difference between her and Pat and we could train her to take Pat's place, if needed. I'm sure she would like to bring Josh down as well."

Peter sat for a few seconds looking at him, then softly said "what a good idea!! I would then be in complete control." Mack stopped eating, poured himself a coffee and said, "too right, you would. "Peter stood up looked at him and said, "finish eating your food, then come out onto my balcony, you know where it is."

Peter went to his balcony which had a table, dining chairs and two very big, nicely made lounge chairs. He sat on one which had a small round table near it *with a cup of coffee on. He took a sip and then sat for a few seconds thinking, took out of his pocket and lit a small Havana, cheroot. Mack came and moved one of the dining chairs nearer to him, lit a cigarette and then said, "well Peter, what do you think?" Peter looked at him, smiled, and said, "I think you may have something we could use to our advantage, if it's done right and organised well." Mack replied, "I have just the team to do it. Could I use your place in France to operate the training and induction?" Peter said, "yes, just let my PA know and she will give you the keys." Mack stood up, nodded, and then left, leaving Peter deep in thought.*

It was a sunny morning in the south of France and Sharon Morre was just awakening from a very deep sleep. She got out of bed, put on a dressing gown, and walked through the door to the kitchen, on the way she looked in a mirror and saw how ruffled her hair was. She filled a kettle to make a cup of tea. She sat at the kitchen table, deep in thought about the man she had met last night. She was already in love and mesmerised by him. Tall, handsome and with dark blue eyes that at times seem to pierce through her. Sharon still felt his kiss and his arms around her, even now. Then the phone rang so she walked over to it on the small table against the wall and said, "Hello." A male voice replied, and she immediately felt weak at the knees as it said, "Sharon are you free today for lunch at 12 noon and then for a trip to the country in the afternoon?"

"Yes, Rob" she replied, and he then said, "see you at the small cafe near the monument, where we went yesterday, at 12 noon" She giggled and then went back to her cup of tea.

Rob turned to Mack standing behind him saying, "she will be there, you are sure she will not be hurt?" Mack gave him a half smile and replied, "that's the last thing we want, in fact as soon as you persuade her to move into the villa, the better, as that will have bodyguards everywhere. Do you think you can convince her to go?" Rob grinned, "of course I do, she's infatuated with me." In that case you had better pack a case and go to the villa to be with her! "Mack ordered and Rob nodded yes.

Mack then rang Peter Morre and updated him on the progress so far with the procurement of Sharon Rodriguez and her infatuation with Rob, who was going to meet her at the French villa. Peter commented "that, this could open a few more possibilities, so keep in touch" He continued to develop the idea he had in his mind on how he could use Sharon to get the shares he needed to control the group. The idea involved a man who was very ingrained in a UK for the British only and was deeply involved in a Neo-Nazi type of organisation, called the National

British Movement (NBM). This was unknown to his partner, Josh.

At this moment Peter was being taken by his driver to an old house on the outskirts of London, set near a wooded area. The house was surrounded by a high brick wall that had electric contact wires on the top that set off alarms, if disturbed and touched in any way. They were monitored in a small room with TV screens and CCTVs. The room was always occupied, and security guards checked the monitors every few hours, patrolling the vicinity 24 hours a day. It was occupied by a person who was employed to keep contact records on everywhere in the house and sur-rounding area. It was known as Wood House! Peter's car stopped at the high metal gate and his driver pressed a button on the intercom. A voice asked who they were.

The driver replied "Peter Morre". The gates then opened, and intercom voice told them to go to the front of the house where a butler would direct Peter to Sir Ralph.

The car slowly drove up to the entrance. Peter went up the steps and rang the bell. An aged butler came to the door, looked at Peter and said, "Follow me this way, sir" and at a slow pace, Peter was taken to the study.

He was greeted by the leader and founder of an organisation based on nationalism. Sir Ralph Walze, MP, a British ex-officer of the army, in fact a colonel of an infantry regiment that had been amalgamated into another regiment due to the reduced need for men, in this modern age!

Sir Ralph was of medium height, with a very bald head and immaculately dressed in a tailored black suit, white shirt, and regimental tie.

He had left the army very dissatisfied with the reduction in manpower and as with likeminded officers; he was given a golden handshake, redundancy and a knighthood. He liked the knighthood but having a tendency towards the Nazi doctoring of Aryan Race, he believed in 'British for Britain'. He had contact with a group of ex-German officers, both old and new, who still worked towards the next rise of Nazism and he often travelled to America to meet them.

Sir Ralph turned from the window and said to Peter, "welcome, I believe you are being looked at by the Monopoly people on your amalgamation?"

Peter looked at him and replied, "Yes we are, it's a normal investigation for amalgamating large businesses and even more so, as they deal with MOD contracts and have a weapons manufacturing ancillary as well!"

Sir Ralph said, "we better be careful though in case they have a MI5 check as well!!"

Peter replied, "We will have to as they will be thorough, so yes, we must be careful with regard to our contact." Sir Ralph ushered him towards the patio doors and said, "let's go onto the balcony for lunch, you can bring me up to speed on everything."

They sat at a table and the butler brought lunch. Peter put him in the picture on everything relating to Pat, her sister, and Peter's intentions, which, Sir Ralph agreed with. They then shook hands and Peter left, feeling content that he was on the right track to sort out his problems in a way that would suit him. Back in his car, he smiled and puffed on his Havana cigar, he had a good feeling and as he looked out of the car window, he noted a black car with a driver sitting in it, as they passed by.

AN UNFORGETTABLE MEMORY

Part 2

CHAPTER 8

The Deceit Starts

Steve arrived at his hotel in London and when checking in, a note was handed to him by the receptionist who had taken a message from Tony asking him to ring him ASAP. He entered his room, sat on the chair near the chest of drawers and rang Tony, who answered very quickly.

Steve said, "Tony is everything ok? The reply was "well yes, but I have had information come my way that Peter Morre's henchman had found Pat's sister, but she has disappeared again!"

Steve asked, "What's your guess on this?" and Tony said, "Well I think Peter Morre has something to do with her disappearance, but I haven't worked out why! I also know from a contact he was seen coming out a house owned by a Sir Ralph Walze, who is suspected of having contact with groups with neo Nazi connotations. He is on the CIA list for being a suspect terrorist. Although, nothing is proven, if they haven't already done so, our MI5 should put him on their list of suspects?"

Steve went silent for a few seconds and then said, "I think before we decide to do anything, let me talk to Mike at MI5. Keep in touch."

Steve then rang Mike at MI5 and he immediately answered the phone. "Hi Steve" he said.

Steve gave him a rundown of what he had arranged with Pat, he gave an update on the twin sister and his suspicion that Peter had kidnapped her, at this stage he was not sure why but Peter had been observed coming out of Sir Ralph's house. Mike replied, you have certainly been busy, the connection with Sir Ralph is something that we did not know." He finished by saying, "Steve I will come back on this, I am meeting 'T' in a minute."

Within a few minutes, Steve's phone rang; it was Mike asking Steve to attend a meeting now with 'T'. Steve had agreed and before he could say any more, Mike butted in with, "good, a car is already on its way to pick you up in a few minutes" and he rang off.

Steve smiled to himself, he typed a quick text to Tony informing him on where he was going and then putting his coat on, he made his way down to reception.

As Steve entered 'T'' s office, he quickly noted who was also there. He sat beside Mike and nearby' was the second in command of MI6, an agent he uses as his right-hand man called Rob, then Jean (Mike's wife) and finally a man who was introduced as Frank from the Monopoly Commission.

Mike started by outlining information received about a suspected MP – a knight who was under suspicion for terrorist activities and connections. He said this individual had received a visit from Peter Morre, whose business organisation was being investigated by MI5 because of a planned amalgamation by his company with another company, who did a lot of MOD supplies for the UK.

Mike looked at Steve and said, "This is why we invited Steve as he is now contracted by the Chair of the company, which is part owned by Peter Morre. The chair is a lady named Pat Morre and her father is Josh Rodriguez." Steve looked at 'T' and said, "I assume everything said on this matter will fall under the official secrets act?" 'T' nodded a yes.

Steve then informed the meeting that he had met Pat Moore and the subsequent actions and arrangements made by his company to protect her. He told them about how she had been approached by one of Peter's henchman and on what had been done since. He reiterated the arrangements to protect and help Pat until the avaricious attempt to get shares off her stops. Finally, he mentioned that it had only been by chance that a colleague who works for him, had gained information of Peter visiting Knights house and had been seen leaving a friend of his.

Frank cut in with, "well, that does not bode well for the amalgamation particularly if we can prove a close contact with knight."

"T replied", "We have agents watching this house and the owners Josh and Peter. Pat, we leave this with you and Steve but please have close cooperation with us and ask us if you need help. Have we found anything else on Pat's twin sister?"

Steve replied there was no news except that she had disappeared again and that he has everyone looking for her.

'T' then said, "I want Jean and Mike to work with you Steve. They can ask questions and check out the amalgamation." He concluded the meeting by thanking everyone who had attended, asked them to stay in touch and to find as much as possible. Everyone then left and as Steve was leaving, Mike said, "let's go to my office Steve and develop a plan of action."

They went to an office that Steve knew well. Following a half hour's discussion, Steve left to go to meet Pat Morre. He walked in, after knocking on her office door and she came towards him, gave him a hug and kissed him on the cheek saying, "I've ordered tea, would you like to join me."

He smiled and said, "That would be lovely. Do you have some time for us to chat?'

At that moment, Pats PA named Sue, came in, smiled, poured their teas and then left. Steve explained that he met with his MI5 contacts, that they had offered to help and that they were working with the monopoly people to check on her firm. He said this was routine for organisations working on MOD contracts now or in future.

Pat replied that as she had mentioned below, she was more than happy for any investigation to take place.

Steve smiled and said, "I have also found out that you have a twin sister?"

She looked at him and he held the smile on his face as she said, "yes, and a skeleton from my father's cupboard." She returned his smile and continued,

"She broke off all family contact when she was

dating a man that the family did not approve of and I've since heard that he has left her. I do not know where or how she is. She cut me out of her life because I had decided to stay with our father, even though I had disagreed with him on cutting her off, she did not deserve that."

Steve replied, "Family squabbles. It happens!" He then quickly changed the subject by asking if she had heard anything from her people regarding the company shares offer. Pat shook her head and said, "no."

Steve then stood up to leave, mentioning that he was meeting Tony in 15 minutes. He asked her if she had any plans for the night and she replied, "No, a night in for a change, you?"

Steve replied that he would probably spend time with Tony finalising things and was pleased that she would be safe at home. They said their good-byes and he left.

Tony had made enquiries with his contacts as to where Sharon, Pats sister, could have disappeared to. He had found out that a Sharon Rodriguez had left on a flight to the South of France with another man and a woman that morning.

He had checked all the flights and was waiting for Steve to arrive.

Steve arrived 15 minutes later at a local bar, their

usual meeting place. Tony had ordered drinks and sandwiches. Tony updated him about Sharon travelling to the south of France and that he had found out that Peter Morre had a holiday villa there.

Steve replied, "Well done Tony, you have been busy. Why do you think she has gone there?" Tony scratched his chin replying, "I'm not sure but it's a big coincidence that it should happen now particularly with all that's going on with Pat and the amalgamation." He also questioned why Sharon who had so far been free to live her life as she wanted should suddenly end up living at Peter's villa?

Steve smiled and said, "Um, Peter obviously has a reason to keep her there but for what, that is the question. Pat has given me no indication that she and her sister, Sharon, don't get on"

Tony replied, "Looks like I may need to fly over and do some investigating?" Steve laughed and said, "What time did you say your flight was?" With a big grin, Tony replied "in an hour and I've packed an overnight bag."

They then stood up, shook hands and went their own ways.

Tony arrived at the airport, the check in for his

flight went smoothly and he was soon boarding the plane. He was seated next to an attractive young lady and they acknowledged each other with smiles. Tony introduced himself as he sat down and said, "I hope you do not mind me reading a book, I have some catching up to do; my trip to France is a business one." She replied, "no problem, I might drop off anyway." So, he got his book out, titled "How to understand shares" and settled down to read it.

The usual safety demonstration was completed by the hostesses and they were soon up in the air. A few minutes later, a stewardess walked up and down the aisle asking if anyone wanted drinks, sandwiches, etc. Tony sighed, put his book on his knee and said, "so, I guess I am not going to get any peace and quiet to read" and turning to the young lady next to him, he asked "would you allow me to get you a drink, I'm having one and I do not like to drink alone?" Smiling she replied, "Thank you, please may I have a gin and tonic."

When the stewardess approached their seats, he ordered two gin and tonics. The lady sitting next to him then introduced herself as "Sue" and they shook hands. He noticed that she had a wedding ring and so he asked, "have you been married long?" She smirked a little and replied about two years and that her husband was an officer in the

Forces and abroad at the moment.

Tony said, "I have an appointment in the South of France for a few days." He then explained that he had never had a holiday in France, and he could not speak French,"

Sue replied that she did speak French as her husband was in the French army and had a weekend pass." Tony smiled and with a glint in his eye, he raised his glass to her and said, "Here's to a nice weekend." "Thank you," she said grinning.

CHAPTER 9

The Search

Tony cleared customs quickly, but Nice airport was busy, so he was a while before he came out to arrival lounge and as he made his way to the exit, he spotted a notice with his name on.

He walked over to a lady who was holding it in front of her face and said, "I'm Tony Brook." She pulled the notice lower and he gasped, saying, Nicola!!

She smiled back replying, "So it is, the Tony I knew in the Forces! I wasn't sure!"

They embraced and he held her at arm's length, and she said, "Sweet dreams." He laughed and replied, "I will now" and at the same time thinking, thank goodness for remembering the code word given by MI5. As they walked together to leave, she said, "Wait here, I will bring the car up". She smiled at him and before she left, she said, "don't talk to any strange women and watch your back," She then quickly walked towards the car park area. He looked around at the busy airport and then heard a female voice say, "Tony."

He turned and standing there holding hands with a man in a French paratrooper uniform was Sue, his co-passenger, from the plane. She said, "Hi Tony, I would like you to meet my husband, Carl." They shook hands and Carl said in perfect English, "pleased to meet you, have you been to Nice before?" Tony murmured, "no, but I have a lady friend who has met me and is fetching the car"

At that moment Nicola pulled up in the car, lowered the car window and smiling at Tony she said, "Get in, we are late." Tony said his goodbyes and got into the car and they sped off onto the highway. Nicola said to him, "I thought I told you not to talk to any ladies?" He laughed and said, "But this one was married and has a husband." They giggled together.

As they drove along, Nicola explained how agents from all over the world were passing through Nice and so people had to be careful who they talked to. She said, "I am taking you to a hotel that has been booked for you" and within 15 minutes they were driving into the hotel's car park.

She got out and said, "I will check you in and accompany to your room.

He put his bag down and looked at her. She looked back at him, and then said, "Tony when you left Berlin, why did you not write to me?"

He stood looking intently stern at her and replied, "my pride!! I could not do it as you had not turned up. I did ring you before I got my train, but you did not answer. So why didn't you write?"

She looked intently at him and said, "The same as you, pride!! You were not there when I had turned up to meet you. I was only 20 minutes late."

He then said turning directly in front of her and explained that he had been ordered on an immediate mission by his unit and had no time to inform or contact her, but he did go to the place they had agreed to meet at. She smiled and said, "well it looks like our occupations took over our feelings." He returned the smile and said, "What a fool I've been. I really do not think I will ever meet anyone so beautiful and so evenly matched to me ever again."

She replied, "me too and my job now makes it much more difficult."

They were standing facing each other and put their arms around each other, then kissed a gentle, lingering one and when they parted, they were both breathless.

They sat down on the bed and Nicola said, "We have found the villa that Sharon, Pat's sister, is staying at, but it appears she is never allowed out on her own. If she goes anywhere, she is always accompanied by someone, but saying this I have booked a table for dinner tonight at a restaurant they go to and if we are lucky, we might see her. The villa is being watched by our agents who report to us on any movement."

She then stood up and said to Tony, "see you at 7pm in reception, a taxi has been ordered, bye, see you later" and then she left.

Tony sat on the bed just thinking and started reminiscing in his thoughts to five years ago about the brief but intense affair he had with Nicola in Berlin.

She had been in the military police and had to attend to a call from the proprietor of the restaurant where he was having a meal with two friends. They had taken part in a successful mission near the city; all three were Lieutenants in the marine commandos, all in civvies.

Their names were Mike and Ray. They were enjoying their first decent meal for four days with lots of wine which had made them tipsy. Ray was chatting up a couple of ladies at a table near them when suddenly; they were joined by their boyfriends who had been held up in traffic. The two boyfriends sensed their girlfriends had been flirting with Ray and made them move round the table, so they had their backs to the three of us.

We just smirked and enjoyed our meal and more wine.

The proprietor, who knew we were in the military, came to our table and spoke to us as he had seen us several times in his establishment.

Everything went ok until, a little tipsy Tony got up to go to the men's room and accidentally knocked one of the boyfriend's arm, making him spill a little wine.

He guy jumped up and as Tony turned to apologise, he was hit with an uppercut followed by a kick in the stomach, which sent him backwards, knocking over an empty table. He hit his head splitting it open and all went black for him a few minutes. Ray and Mike were in like a shot and the men were pinned down, unable to move when the military police came in.

They took statements from the men and Nicola and a military police male picked Tony up and took him to the military hospital in the barracks nearby.

Ray and Mike followed in their car driven by a military policeman.

Nicola took Tony in and as he passed a mirror, all he could see was a bloody face looking back.

Tony was kept in overnight in case of concussion and the next day Nicola came to see him to take a statement. From memory, he was dozing when she came into his room and spoke to him. He opened his eyes and thought it was an angel who had come for him; she looked so attractive in civvies. Their relationship bloomed and both fell in love with each other, but their brief affair only lasted just over a month.

It was a grey September day five years ago when they were parted and a coincidence of being on the same case had brought them back together. He sighed and stood up looking forward to their evening together, although it was still working on the Morre case.

CHAPTER 10

Love and Investigation

In London, Steve had been busy investigating Peter Morre's activities with

Sir Ralph and Mike had found out a contact of Sir Ralphs in America.

This person was a son of a German who had immigrated to the USA after the war in the 1950s.

The son had been educated at Harvard University, had a degree in finance and became well known in the financial circles as a very good forecaster of estimated and future financial forecasts. He had built up his own company on this reputation.

Having achieved all this and so much more at University but he fell out of favour with his father, who had been a General in the Nazi regime and knew all about the loss of life and industry that the Second World War had produced.

He still held very dear his Nazi beliefs, which his

son did not share, in fact, the son was a staunch USA believer in his living and even served in Vietnam on being drafted.

Mike had met him at a chamber of commerce dinner a few nights back.

He was apparently in his cups but was going on about the Nazi sympathisers on the news that evening, who were getting stronger and he said, "if they were like his father, there was no way you could change his mind and he had heard a Sir someone or other had given a speech at their last meeting on the growing numbers they are now getting in the UK."

Mike had agreed with him and managed to get out of him where the group his father belonged to hold their meetings. Mike had then contacted the CIA who were grateful for the information, they kept an eye on the father and kept Mike posted on progress.

Steve had just entered Pat Morre's office. He had been contacted by her PA to meet Pat at 10am on this cloudy and very fresh morning in London.

She welcomed him with a hug and a peck on the cheek and they both sat down, she sat behind the desk and he sat opposite her in front of the desk. They both had a cup of tea as she knew that they both had the same tastes this time of day.

She took a sip of her tea, smiled and said to him, "I have been invited to a meeting with Peter and my Father, Josh, at 10.30 am. Can you attend with me?" He put his cup down smirked and said, "To right, I can, I've been hoping that I would meet them. Do you want me to just be silent unless they get threatening and how will you introduce me?"

She smiled with that look she sometimes gave of innocence, saying, "You are my very good friend and adviser and my escort!" Steve giggled and replied, "Sounds good to me."

"To get there," she commented, "will take about 15 minutes, so drink up. I have a car waiting to take us.

Also, Steve can you escort me also to a chamber of commerce dinner this evening? I can have a car to pick you up from your hotel at 7pm tonight, please?" and gave him a nice smile, so he retorted, "Certainly, how can I refuse!!"

On the way in the car she snuggled up to him and said, "I have missed you in the last day or so." She gave him another nice smile and soon they had arrived.

On entering Peter's office, Steve took a quick survey of the room from his military training habit. A large desk, bookshelves, full of a variety of books, five chairs positioned with one behind the desk that was occupied by Peter. There was a chair on either side of the desk; one was occupied by Josh and the other one by Joe Morre, Pat's ex-husband. The rest of the office had filing cabinets and a small bar. The widows were open, and Peter was puffing on his Havana cigar.

He started the conversation with "welcome Pat. You know who we are, would you like to introduce your escort, please!!"

Pat looked at me with a smirk on her face and said, "this is my friend, adviser and escort, Steve Long, owner of Longs Private Investigation Company." She turned to Steve and introduced Peter Morre as her ex father in law, Joe, her ex-husband and Josh Rodriguez, her father. Steve looked at them, nodded and said," Hello."

Peter explained about the proposed amalgamation and that they wanted to buy Pat's shares and that she should be selling them back to the main shareholding in the group as it had taken many years for the main shareholders to build up.

He explained that they were not trying to deprive Pat of the Chair of the group but by them not being the main shareholders, it had put them in a position of someone else having more say in the direction of the group and they were not willing for that to happen.

Pat interjected her father Josh and said, "Do you think this as well." He did not look her in the eyes and said, "Yes I feel Peter and I should be equal and the main shareholders."

Pat then replied, "well gentlemen, I have contracted a firm to negotiate this matter on my behalf, so I do not intend to discuss it with you today. Please can you discuss it with them?"

Joe said, "I don't think it's wise of you to do that!"

Pat felt Steve twitch, as though he was going to say something to Joe.

She put her hand on his, squeezed it and staring at Joe angrily, she said, "I have just explained what I want, and I hope Joe that was not a threat?" Joe looked at her and stuttered, "No, it was not meant as such!!"

Peter jumped in and said, "There is no threat, but you will put Pat in a difficult position if you don't sort it and I'm not someone who likes to be put in that position."

Steve could hold back no longer and he continued by saying, "please note I have remembered what you have just said and I consider it a veiled threat and I, as Pat's protector and adviser, take objection to that.

I have a good memory and shall record it, and please note, should any harm be intimated at Pat, it is un-

acceptable and will be met with the full force of the law."

Pat and Steve then stood up and walked out the office. As they walked towards the entrance of the building, they met the CEO of the group, a lady called Sandra Hand.

Pat and Steve gave her a quick review of what had just happened with the other main share-holders and Pat's answer. The CEO said, "Well, I am warned and will watch my back as well, I will keep in touch." She then smiled and walked away down the corridor.

Pat and Steve drove off in the chauffer driven car,

Back in Peter's office, before he left, Josh said to Peter and Joe, "don't push Pat too far, you heard her, she is prepared to fight you and that will not get you the shares.".

Peter spoke on his intercom and asked his PA "get me Mack please. I want to speak to him now!" Joe stood up to leave but Peter told him to stay.

Mack knocked on the door, entered the office, sat down and said "hello".

Peter replied,"

"how is our plan at the villa going, is Sharon doing what we want her to?" Mack gave one of

his grins which looked more of a snarl and said,"
"yes, she is, and she is also doing well on copying
Pat's signature. It seems she really hates Josh and
wants to get back at him."

*Peter had a draw on his cigar, letting the smoke out
his lips slowly then turned to Mack and asked," how
long before she is ready?" Mack replied "I think another day and she should be able to pass off as Pat! In
fact this evening, she and her team are going out for
a meal in a restaurant that she likes and they do not
know that she is not Pat, so it will be a good try out of
how well she has progressed." "Good, keep in touch"
replied Peter.*

At his hotel in Nice, Tony was waiting in the reception area at 6.45 pm in a blazer, grey trousers
and a tie. He began reading an English newspaper
when a very tall, black male with a peeked cap
came up to him and said in English with a very
slight French accent, "sir, I am your taxi driver
and there is a lady in the car, waiting outside."
Tony followed him to a large dark Citron car. He
opened the door, and Tony got in, smiled at Nicola and gave her a kiss on the cheek. He thought
she smelt lovely as he said, "good evening".

Nicola smiled back and said, "the restaurant is
not far. Sid, my driver, knows the place and will

wait for us if we need him." Tony nodded yes.

When they arrived, Sid opened the car door for them and as they stepped out, Tony noticed Nicola's shoulder length black hair, her tight-fitting long dress and the sparkling necklace on her tanned skin. He said, "you look as beautiful as I remember you always did" and to his surprise she flashed a smile and with a twinkle in her eyes and replied, "and you still scrub up well"

A waiter took them to their table and sat them opposite an unoccupied table set for 6 people.

They ordered their wine and meal and were both being hungry after a hectic day.

Their talked about the purpose of Tony's visit to Nice, the unknown reason for Sharon's sudden interest in the Morre family and questions about her sudden residence in the villa in France.

Nicola informed him that they had a MI5 agent working in the villa which was having a lot of refurbishments works done at the moment. She then suddenly lowered her voice and said, "Talk of the devil, don't look but Sharon and an entourage have just sat at a table opposite to us."

Tony casually reached for the wine and tactfully looked across at the table next to them. Sharon looked identical to Pat Morre!

Nicola said to Tony, "this could be a very interesting evening! If she goes to the ladies, I will follow and try and get an invitation to meet them all." Tony nodded his approval.

They continued to enjoy their meal and jokingly, referred to places and enjoyment they had together in the past. After about an hour into their meal, they discussed ways of getting introduced to Sharon's table and just then Sharon and another lady from the group, stood up and walked towards the lady's room. Nicola followed them.

Tony sipped his wine, he was nervous, hoping that Nicola would be ok. He needn't have worried as soon, all three of the women returned, laughing and giggling. They stopped near Tony's seat and Nicola introduced him as her partner and introduced Sharon as Pat Morre, the well-known industrialist and Chair of a large group in London who was in Nice on a holiday. Tony stood up and shook Sharon's hand. He said it was a pleasure to meet her and that he had recently read about her rise to fame. He thought it was amazing how well Sharon had managed to copy all the mannerisms and the voice of Pat Moore!

Sharon and the lady who had been with her went back to their seats and Nicola whispered to Tony, "now we know what Sharon is doing in the villa!"

She continued,

"I could not get her to let us join their table; she went very cagey when I asked. Maybe they are controlling her. She seemed frightened."

At that moment, a waiter went up and said something to Sharon's table and they all stood up to leave. On her way out, Sharon waved goodbye to Nicola and Tony, they smiled and waved back. They then looked at each other, stood up, left some money on the table to cover their bill and left the restaurant.

CHAPTER 11

The Kidnapping

In London, Steve had escorted Pat to the Chamber of Commerce dinner. They had dutifully listened to the speeches, enjoyed a good meal with plenty of wine and were now standing on a patio terrace cooling down from the crowded function room they had been in.

Steve had his arm on her shoulder, and they were both gazing at the sky and the full moon. It was not yet pitch black and they could distinguish the outlines of plants and trees and smell their fragrance in the air.

Steve gently squeezed her to him and as he relaxed, he suddenly stiffened as he felt a gun in his back. A calm male voice quietly said in his ear, "relax, do as you're told, and no one will get hurt."

Pat froze at the same time because a female standing next to her had put a gun to her back and softly gave her the same instructions. They were then both checked to see if they were armed.

Another male appeared with their coats and they were quietly ushered outside to waiting black car that had its motor running.

They were pushed into the back of the car, the man with the gun sat next to Steve and the female sat in the front with a gun in her hand. The driver sped off down the gravel drive followed by another car onto the main road.

The car had tinted windows and so it was hard to see where they were being taken to. Steve had timed the journey to about ninety minutes. No one had spoken and when they finally arrived at their destination, the male with the gun said, "please get out and behave, no tricks and you will be treated well." The four of them got out and walked to a door that was already open for them.

In Nice, Tony and Nicola were both on their iPods informing their superiors of their findings on Sharon and their opinions that she apparently was being trained to replace Pat and this bode no good to Pat, as it meant she could be replaced by her sister, who looks and speaks like her, plus if she can forge her signature, there would be no stopping her taking over all Pat's business, given half the chance!

Tony was sending his message to Steve and to Mike of MI5.

He finished his email by asking what they wanted him to do now in Nice.

He then heard a knock on his hotel room door and asked who it was. A voice answered, "Nicola, can we speak?" Tony opened his door; she came in and sat on the bed, looking very worried. He said, "Nicola is there a problem?" She replied, "Steve and Pat have disappeared." He jumped up off the bed saying, "When?" And she replied "About half an hour ago, around the time Sharon and her entourage left the restaurant"

At that moment, his mobile phone rang, and he said, "hi Mike" then after a minute listening he said, "Ok, I will keep in touch."

He then sat beside Nicola and gave her a brief run down on how Pat's chauffeur, Sam, had gone to check on them, found out they had gone on the terrace for fresh air but then apparently disappeared. He had found on the floor a small piece of a bracelet that Pat had been wearing. Since then, nothing had been heard and the tracker that Steve carried must have been found. Mike had suggested that the villa should be watched just in case; Steve and Pat were taken there.

Nicola used her mobile to update her contacts at the villa and asked them to report back to her if there was any suspicious activity and to tail Sharon, particularly if she left the villa.

Tony turned to Nicola and told her that Mike had asked him to stay in Nice and to update him on the movements in and out of the villa.

Nicola replied, "I will arrange for you to accompany me to a place that we have here that provides intelligence reports that our agents prepare on the villa." He looked at her and said, "that would be good. I think I should go to the villa tonight to see if I can find out anything." She quickly answered "give me ten minutes to change. I will arrange the visit but I'm coming with you." He nodded yes and she left.

He then changed into all black attire and put on a long raincoat.

Nicola had rung him and asked that he meet her at the front parking spaces of the hotel. As he waited, he saw a car draw up with Nicola driving it.

Mike had informed 'T' and had set in motion a full-scale red alert and the MI5 and MI6 agents would be prepared and ready when required.

The house where the Chamber of Commerce dinner had been held had been searched by a Forensic Team, led by Rob, an MI6 agent and who knew

Steve and Mike well. Special Branch was also on alert and was trying to trace the two cars that had left before other cars. Their number plates had been captured from CCTV cameras.

Inside the house that Steve and Pat had been taken to, they were told to go to two bedrooms that had been allocated to them and instructed to change into clothes that had been provided. Steve went to the bathroom and noticed that his shaving and other items were there plus all the medication he needed to stay alive and well. Steve realised that they had been to his hotel room for those items and hence they must have contacts everywhere.

After 10 minutes, a man came to the door to escort Steve to go to the to the lounge downstairs and on their way they met Nicola who was coming out her room with the female, who had sat in the front of the car.

Pat put her arm in his and they walked down and entered the lounge which had a three seated settee, two huge chairs, small tables and other chairs dotted around the room. There was also a cocktail cabinet stocked with a variety of alcoholic drinks.

As they walked in, they noticed a tall bearded male with receding hair and immaculately dressed in a suit. Steve smiled to himself thinking, all that man needed was a monocle and a stick and then they would have gone back to the days when the master of the estate and the house was bullying the work people to listen!

On their arrival, the man stood up and pointing to the settee, he said, "please take a seat." Steve and Pat sat down on the settee.

He introduced himself, "my name is to remain anonymous, but you can call me Colonel." He grunted, "everyone else does. My people have brought you to my estate where you will be detained until the shares and amalgamation of the

R&M Group are sorted to our advantage. We have no intention of harming you unless you force us to do so. Your accommodation is up to your standard and you have freedom to use the rear garden area, but I must warn you, do not to try to escape as all movement is monitored and trust me, you will not succeed.

You both will live in the wing of the house where you can be free to walk about but if you try to escape, again, I warn you, the house has 24/7 surveillance and security guards.

My advice to you is be sensible, don't try to escape, use the time as some sort of break for a few days." He then looked at Pat and giving her a false smile, he said, "of course all of this could be avoided if you had just signed over the transfer of your shares, you know you will get an extremely good price for them and so, if you were to accept, you both could be back home in two days, none the worse for wear." He then chuckled to himself.

Pat looked at him with anger on her face and said, "I might have considered the shares offer but now that you have imprisoned us, you can go to hell!" He replied, "Not yet dear, but maybe Hell might beckon me some day!" He chuckled again.

Steve had remained quiet listening to the conversation and then he said, "Colonel, you cannot get anywhere without Pat's signature and you need her presence to do this!" The Colonel chuckled again and replied, "we have our ways!" He then stood up and said, "if you want a drink, pull this bell cord and someone will come in to serve you or you can just go to your room, as you wish." He then shrugged and left the lounge.

Steve said to Pat, "we are prisoners here and I believe that they have the means to get your shares and forge your signature. I think he knows that if either of us is harmed, it would cause them lots of problems and they could also probably lose the amalgamation. So, they will somehow do it by replacing you. I think he has your sister Sharon!"

Pat gave a 'sharp' intake of breath and then replied, "Sharon! I thought she was dead?" Steve looked at her, he pretended that he was going to kiss her cheek and whispered in her ear, "I think we need to be careful what we say in this house as all the rooms are probably bugged." Then in a louder voice, he said, "would you like a drink, we could perhaps have one on your terrace?"

He got up and pulled the cord which rang the bell.

A female came in and he ordered two coffees and asked if they could be taken to Pat's bedroom terrace. The female said, "yes sir" and left. So, they both made their way to the terrace at the rear of Pat's bedroom. Steve did a quick search to see if her room was bugged and was satisfied that they were no bugs. He took two chairs and placed them as close as he could near the stone fence around the terrace, so that they could freely talk.

Steve started off by saying, "I think by now MI5 and the police will be looking for us as your chauffer would have raised the alarm." Pat was holding two cups of coffee which had been brought up to the room, she was sipping hers, so just nodded yes. She put the cups on a small coffee table she had moved near the chairs. She agreed that alarm bells would have been raised about their disappearance and that

Sharon being alive made sense. She feared that her sister would be very bitter towards her but more so towards their father. Pat told Steve she realised that if her sister was willing to impersonate her, then that puts her in a very dangerous position indeed. Steve looked at her, held her hand and said, "well, I have faith in my people and the authorities and I'm sure they will do everything humanely possible to find us. So, we cooperate up to the point of holding back on signing anything. In the meantime, we have to face and take everything they say and do as it comes. Let's get some sleep and see what tomorrow brings us."

CHAPTER 12

The Search

Tony and Nicola arrived at a small cottage in Nice, France. Nicola had directed Tony to it. Apparently, it was a base that both, MI5 and the French secret service used to cover Nice and now, the villa, which was also under surveillance by the British and the DGES (Direction -General for External Security), the French Secret Service.

They entered a room that had CCTV cameras covering different areas and places. Nicola walked towards a tall, muscular, broad shouldered male and said "Tony, may I introduce you to my main French agent and coordinator on this case." The man turned and smiled at Nicola and then looking at Tony, his smile broadened. Tony suddenly realised that the man was Captain Carl, Sue's husband. Sue was the passenger he had sat next to on the flight earlier.

They both shook hands with a firm grip and Tony

said, "it certainly is a small world." Turning to Nicola, Tony explained how he had met Carl. Nicola was pleased and said, "Good we will make a great team, the Captain is accompanying us on the visit to the Villa."

Carl updated them on his team of agents and a squad of armed police, specially trained in this type of work who would be providing specialist support. He also pointed out the French secret service had evidence of a Nazi type connection and they wanted to sort this out this as well.

They set off in two black Citron cars and on the way, Carl explained to Tony that his people who were staking out the villa had reported two cars driving away from it, about the same time as Tony had received his information of the suspected abduction of Steve and Pat.

Tony commented that it could have been them transferring Sharon, Pat's sister, to England, to impersonate Pat. He said the secret service in the UK was urgently waiting for confirmation on this so that they could block this attempt.

They arrived at the gates of the villa and after a short exchange of words with Carl, the gates opened, and they were followed by an armed squad who knocked on the front door and then rang a bell. The door was opened by a butler of sorts who took then through to the lounge where a manager was waiting to inspect their paperwork to search the place. Carl took control and left the warrant with the manager. The agents, Tony, Nicola and the armed police began a search.

Within half an hour into the search, Tony, Nicola and Carl were convinced that Sharon had been moved to somewhere else by the people controlling her.

Carl commented that the Sharon/Pat issue was a problem for the UK. During the search of the villa, they discovered a room that was locked and when they opened it, they saw it was some sort of meeting room with Nazi swastika flags, other sort of items and a list of people who were associated to this organisation.

Tony rang Mike at MI5 and informed him of what they had found and Mike said, "Tony I agree with your assumption about the replacing of Pat by these people and that this will be put into operation here in the UK.

I've put out an alert to all airports, docks, trains, etc. to watch out for them. As for the Nazi connection, that now might be proof of Peter Morre's connection to it. Also, tell Nicola to stand ready for a call from MI6 on her next connection to this case. I suggest you both get some sleep and a breakfast and wait for further instructions." He then cut off.

Tony related the conversation to Nicola and Carl. Nicola then asked Carl to send his info on the raid to MI5 and suggested that they head back to the hotel for breakfast. Tony nodded yes.

Arriving back at the hotel they found out breakfast would start in half an hour, so they went to their rooms, changed out of the all black attire and arrived in the dining room just as it was opening up for breakfast. They ordered a full English breakfast, toast and tea.

After they sat down, Nicola said to Tony, "what do you think will happen now?"

He looked at her in the eyes thinking she was near to tears and said "I guess whatever it is, could mean us parting again, after all it is our jobs, and this will always happen. Nicola, I want to say what I must say and that is, I do not intend to make our parting forever this time and would like us to keep in contact."

She held his hand and squeezed it gently replying breathlessly, "Tony, so do I."

They smiled at each other and let go of their hands as the meal came.

Halfway through breakfast both their phones

rang, so they answered them.

Five minutes later they put their phones down and Steve said, "that was Mike of MI5. I have to stay couple more days to help you and you are to give me instructions on what we need to do."

Nicola smiled and replied, "Yes, my instructions are to investigate the villa's dark secrets especially after we found the room with the Nazi connotations in it. I'm glad we will have more time together!" He agreed that was the gist he had got and that they might be joined by two Israeli's, who would investigate all Nazi type of organisations. Mike also said he had the full force of the secret services to find and sort Steve and Pat's disappearance and that they were also aware of the possibility of Sharon replacing Pat.

They had finished breakfast by this time, so Pat left Steve for a few seconds to ring the MI6 contingent in the Nice area to arrange transport and two trackers.

By this time the sun had come out signalling a warm day ahead, traffic was building up on the roads, the sounds of the early hustle and bustle of noise had begun, to say another day had arrived.

Nicola's usual driver pulled up at the hotel entrance, they both got in and the car sped off to the villa. When they arrived, the front door was opened by the police guard and they went to the lounge

Carl and one of his agents were sifting through a pile of papers on the desk. Nicola said, "hello Carl, we are back to continue where we left off yesterday as it seems my head of MI6 in London wants me to investigate the inference of a Nazi connection and to find out how involved the owner, Peter Morre, is in it."

Carl replied, "so I believe. I had an email you would be back, how can I help?"

Nicola commented that she could start by having a closer look at the room with the Nazi flags and mementos. Carl said, "be my guest, you know where the room is."

She and Tony went to the room. Tony found a camera installed in the air conditioning in the ceiling and when he searched the desk, he found a secret drawer within one of the bigger drawers. Inside it were papers which he placed on the desk and soon realised, that one contained a list of people names and emails. He showed it to Nicola who said, "we can get our people to check them out." She then recognised two names of people who operated in the Nice area, not far from the villa and so suggested that they could perhaps pay them a visit. Tony smiled and agreed that they needed to find out what sort of people were in the organisation and what they were doing? Nicola notified Carl where they were going, and they then left.

CHAPTER 13

The Search

On the outskirts of London in a large walled house, Steve and Pat sat on the terrace talking about their abduction; both realising MI5 would be using their considerable resources to find them.

Steve had carefully considered all the possibilities of them being found and hoped that it would be soon. He knew that if the kidnappers were going to use Sharon to impersonate Pat, then they would have to work hard to make it work so no suspicions were raised. He worried however that the longer all this took, the more dangerous it would be for Pat and himself and he feared that their lives would be at serious risk. He had prepared a plan to get to know the garden area that they were allowed to walk in and he wanted to explore as much of it as possible by insisting they need to exercise and walk in the fresh air.

When they went down to breakfast together, they asked the butler come gofer!! if they could they walk in the garden for fresh air and exercise?

He left the room and came back to inform them that they could go for a walk but asked that they keep away from the wall and gates as those were electrified and if touched, would give a nasty shock. They both nodded yes, and he left.

Half an hour later they were in their coats, slowly walking on the paths around the garden, making it able to talk easier away from the room bugs, several of which Steve had found in each bedroom.

Pat said to Steve, "do you think they intend to harm us." He put his arm around her shoulders and carefully said, "I don't think so, not yet! But it depends how much your sister can fool everyone. To be honest I cannot understand yet why they have abducted us and not just made us disappear?"

Pat replied, "yes, I was thinking the same, also if Sharon succeeds, then they don't need us, if she fails, then they don't need her."

Steve turned, looked her in the face and said, "is there anything you deal with that would require your fingerprint or an eye scan?"

Pat replied that she had to use an eye scan at the bank for certain things and a hand scan for some records in the development department.

He then told her what he had thought this morning in his room. He was sitting at the dresser mulling over his and Pat's position in the plan of action, "maybe our captors plan is to probably replace Pat with her twin sister!"

He continued, "There was no point abducting him with Pat and keeping them both alive, if they intended the swop to be successful, as they must know the authorities would have a full alert all over the world looking out for them. Considering this, it would point to their abductors using them in a fall back way, of being of some use, if their plan failed."

Steve had rubbed his chin in a quandary until he said out loud to himself, looking in the mirror, "of course, they think Pat and I are involved with each other!"

He continued his deliberations, and decided, he was the one they would use to convince the authorities and the firm that they had eloped together and so Sharon her sister, could appear for work after having a romantic few days with her lover.

Also, if needed, they could force Pat to relinquish some shares to stop them killing him! Again, he had rubbed his chin, looked in the mirror at himself, shrugged, smiled and said aloud, "yes, that's what they think!"

Pat replied "and they would be right, I would not let you be harmed"

Steve squeezed her and said, "thank you and I would

not willingly let them harm you either but unfortunately they control us at the moment, so we must not show we fear anything from them."

By this time, they had walked around the garden, so they chose a seat near the path to sit and talk further.

Pat said, "If what you think is true and if their plan succeeds, what do you think will happen to us?"

Steve looked at her in silence for 30 seconds and then replied, "We probably would just disappear somehow!" Pat slowly said, "you mean, killed!!" Steve nodded yes.

So, she retorted, "then what is our plan to be?" He smiled and said, "Go along with them and find some way to fool them into thinking that we believe they are not going to harm us." Pat sighed and said, "Ok?"

They both started to stand up and noticed the butler coming along the path and he said, "Would you be good enough to go to the library please."

They both nodded yes and went to the library and the male soft voice gunman was sitting behind the desk. He asked them to sit down and then said he wanted Steve to send a note informing his firm he was taking a short break with Pat and would be in touch later. Steve looked at him and said, "I guess this is to stop people looking for us?" Steve then in-

sisted "I want some assurance you intend no harm to us if I do, otherwise you can forget it! I know eventually they will find us, do not kid your self as we both are in regular contact with organisations and people, who will make it their job to find us, alive or dead."

Steve looked him in the eyes and could see the steely glint of a man who would not flinch at doing the latter.

'Grim –face' as Pat, had named him, cracked into a slight grimace for a smile and replied, "My instructions are to keep you both in good health, so I can give you the assurance without any hesitation."

Steve looked at Pat, who nodded ok, so he stood up, picked up a sheet of paper and wrote a short note

Dear Tony

Just to let you know that Pat and I are ok and enjoying a short time together.

I expect you to keep the business going of course and work on our case in London. I'm sure you can sort that out according to what we had discussed.

Tell Mike at MI5 that I'm ok and I will contact him on my return.

Regards,
Steve Long

He gave the note to 'grim- face' to read, and as expected, he grimaced and said, "thank you, you can now get on with your day."
Steve said, "Address it to Tony Brook"

Pat and Steve left the room and returned to the terrace outside Pat's room.

He put an arm around Pat and whispered in her ear, "Tony will read in between the lines and will realise that the note was done under duress, so let's keep our fingers crossed.

It's going to be a boring day ahead with not a lot to do, so how about getting a couple of books from the library to read".

CHAPTER 14

The Search Continues

In the afternoon, Steve's PA saw that a note had been pushed through the letterbox, addressed to Tony. She then rang a number she had to contact him. He answered and asked her to read it to him. Tony then gave her his other email address to send it to, so she printed it off for filing. Within half an hour, he had received it. It was in Steve's handwriting without a doubt.

Tony was in an office with Nicola. He showed her the email and said, "they have made a mistake in making him send this note as the bit about London was a case he was dealing with which I think he wanted to keep undercover, so points to the fact that he has been abducted. He is not on a romantic break with Pat. He is one person who would not do that, while working on a case."

Nicola looked at him and replied that Steve should talk to Mike at MI5.

Tony nodded yes, smiled and rang Mike on his

private number that only a few people had.

A woman answered, "Hello, its Jean. Tony, what can I do for you?"

Tony explained that he had received Steve's note and his deductions on the content. Mikes wife, Jean, who worked with him at MI5, then replied, "I will contact Mike and I'm sure he will get straight back to you, I think you are right in your deduction."

Nicola could not get any contact from the people she wanted to talk to, so she and Tony went a walk in the sun and to look at the bay and boats in their moorings. The air was filled with a mixture of sea scent and diesel fumes, plus cooking smells from the small restaurants that were dotted along the front. They stopped at one of them that Nicola had visited before, sat down at a table, and ordered two gin and tonics and sandwiches. Tony said, "this is the life, no rushing around and sunny weather to sit and enjoy a snack and drink." Nicola smiled that smile that would melt any man's reserve and nodded a yes. She replied, "Enjoy while you can as we never know when they will want us elsewhere and I feel they will want you back in London to find Steve." Tony looked at her with no smile on his face and commented that he thought she was right, but somehow, he will find a way for them to get together.

She held his hand and said to him looking directly at him, "do you really mean it this time?" He kissed her very tenderly and when they parted looked into her eyes nodded and said, "Yes."

Tony's phone rang and he answered it saying, "hi Mike, thanks for the quick return call."

Mike said that he agreed with Tony that Steve was being held by someone and had written the note under duress as he would never disappear and make no contact, especially as he knew his commitment to them and other people.

He said they should continue to look for them but not get any media people involved so that the captors would think their plan was working. He mentioned that they must have taken Steve's watch as he had one with a tracker in, but it was not showing up anywhere.

He said he also thought Mike and Nicola should continue to investigate the fascist connections in Nice and that he would arrange if needed to keep both him and Nicola as a team. He coughed and remarked quickly, "I do remember when you both first met and what happened, so I will keep you together as long as possible. Let's talk later when I've informed 'T'. Speak soon" and then he cut off.

Tony related the conversation to Nicola who replied by saying, "I will ask my contacts to start finding the people we need to talk to, so let's get back to my office."

In London's MI5 headquarters, Mike, Jean and 'T' were discussing the disappearance of Steve and Pat and the implications if Sharon, her sister, was used to take Pat's position. It transpired there was not any way except by their different manner of talking and mannerisms, which they were sure, would have been carefully synchronised, to appear exactly the same as Pat's.

"So, this would be a problem," 'T' grunted. He wanted a full-scale search done to find them, and every police and government resources should be used. He had no doubt that this case had a deeper meaning of terrorism, Nazi connotations and money ideals than how it appeared at the moment. He also agreed with Mike that it was important for Tony and Nicola to get more information on the findings in the villa.

'T' had put a "For Your Eyes Only" notice on the case so it was classed as top secret, only certain ranks would have access to the information. It was officially Mike's case with Jean, as his second in command. Mike had obtained the service of a very good chief police inspector called Dave Wall and Pete Alward, who was a sergeant. They were both very experienced in finding people and had more contacts than an electric circuit box!

At the moment all the cameras in the area of the building where Pat and Steve had been taken from were being viewed by very experienced people who could normally spot items that Mike and others would have missed.

Mike was determined to find Steve and Pat, being inwardly aware they would be killed in an accident or something else, once their use had expired.

He had put himself back in the field of operations to personally make sure this did not happen.

Jean his wife knew the signs. Mike was determined to sort this, and she was going to support him.

The visitors list was being scrutinised to see if anyone fitted a profile of an abductor. Mike walked into the department dealing with the CCTV photos and bumped into the chauffer, who had driven Steve and Pat to the dinner. The chauffer was looking at the cars coming and going from the dinner building. He was introduced to Mike and said that if he spotted the car, he would recognise them, but so far, no luck. Mike just said, "well, keep me informed."

In the large walled house, Pat and Steve were taking a walk again and trying to face their position with knowledge of having to obey them but still being their own masters. They were being treated well; they could go for walks and watch TV. Steve informed Pat that she must be steadfast in denying them her signature or anything else that would take her and Steve's usefulness away from them as they both were well aware, their usefulness was the only thing that was keeping them alive.

Steve, unknown to Pat, had a plan to use his trained stealth he had to get around the place later this evening when everyone should be asleep. The evening came. Steve and Pat watched TV for a time, then both retired to their bedrooms and Pat went to bed.

Steve found some dark clothes and waited until he heard the doors downstairs being locked. He gave it another half an hour, then silently slipped out of his room and carefully went downstairs. He went to the rear double glass doors and using a knife slowly opened them, observing that the bit of plastic he put in the circuit earlier was still there, so the alarm was neutralized. He very carefully walked around the outside of the house. Good, no dogs he thought, one room higher up had a light on, but he had no idea who it was in that room. He got to the front of the building and there were three cars there. He made a note of their number plates.

Then using the shrubs for cover, he went down the side of the road to the front gates. By the look of them they relied on a camera and a visitor intercom.

He then retraced his steps back to the front door, turned right along the path around the house and suddenly as he turned the corner, he had to dive into the shrubs, as two men came out of a side door talking and laughing as they walked up the path to the front drive. As they walked past, Steve smelt cigarette smoke.

He moved silently, staying in the shrubs up to the door they had come out. He carefully tried the door and it opened into a small room full of CCTV equipment, with about twelve screens, all labelled to indicate the area monitored.

He looked at one marked as his bedroom and thought he had made a good job of rolling cushions and pillows under the covers to make a shape of a body. He then clicked onto Pats bedroom and she was fast asleep on her side. He thought it was pretty poor that the security staff that was monitoring these cameras had both left the room at the same time. Then Steve moved to the inner door, tried it and to his surprise, it opened!!

So, he slipped out into the corridor and went towards the next door, he opened it and it was adjourning the main entrance foyer. He stepped into the foyer and walked to the stairs, and then very slowly and carefully, he started to climb them. At the top of them, he turned right and soon came to his bedroom door.

Steve examined it to see if it was wired for an alarm and did not find one, so having had the forethought to have put his door key in his pocket, he used it to open the door and went back into his bedroom, took out the cushions and pillows and went to the terrace. He sat on a chair and was soon deep in thought.

He said to himself, "well they are not equipped to keep people in but to keep them out." He watched dawn start and fell asleep in this position.

He woke up stiff everywhere on his body, so he had a hot shower which made him feel better. He got dressed and was ready for breakfast

CHAPTER 15

Another Problem

Another day was starting in London the air was cooler and some leaves had started to change their colour on some bushes and trees'

Peter was on his way to his London office and was being driven by his faithful chauffer dressed in his grey suit and tie. His hat was on his nearside seat for when he alighted and opened doors.

Peter was puffing on his Havana cigar, very much in thought on how the amalgamation was stuck and waiting for the monopoly people who were taking their time to give a verdict. They arrived at his office car park and he got out from the car and went straight to his office saying hello to people as he passed them.

Seated behind his desk he spoke into the intercom and asked his PA to send Mack in, when he arrived. He then picked up his mobile and rang Joe, his son and left a message to contact him as soon as he could.

A knock came on his door, Mack walked in and Peter told him to sit.

Peter said, "I want an update on what is happening with your scheme to getting Sharon Rodriguez trained.

Mack looked at Peter and replied, "Boss, things have started to move on this, but I will only give you a brief indication of the events now in progress. The training is complete, and steps have been taken to test the daughter out; this is all I can say, lest you are questioned by the Police or MI5. You will then have no connection to what is happening as far as it can be possibly proven."

Peter looked at him, puffing away on his cigar then slowly gave a grimace more than a smile and commented, "I need to know that everyone, including Pat, is safe and no harm as come to her?"

Mack reassured him "I can guarantee Pat and her friend are ok and safe. Sharon is fully ready and trained to replace Pat. We are going to organise a meeting for Sharon to act as Pat, with people who know Pat. This will then indicate if Sharon can pull it off. I'm afraid for your own sake Boss, that's all I can say."

Peter nodded and said, "thanks Mack, I appreciate that, ok, keep in touch."

Mack left.

Peter sat there in thought, wondering who and where they will get Sharon to act as Pat. It had to be at a place where people know Pat. It will be interesting to see if it works, so good luck to them.

After Mack left Peter's office, he drove to the house where the two hostages, Pat and Steve, were being held. On arrival, he met the male and woman who had done the successful hostage taking.

Mack had got these two in, as they were both top professionals, and successful at this sort of thing, very trustworthy, but also very expensive.

No names were ever used even when addressing each other, unless it was a nick name someone wanted to use like Mack did, calling the male, Clyde and the female, Bonnie. Mack thought this clever and it confused people.

"well then, Clyde how are things going?"- asked Mack!

The male in his very soft voice replied, "Everything has gone as planned and a note has been sent to his colleague informing that Pat and he are having a romantic weekend.

Also, we aim today or tomorrow to take Pat away for a day and replace her with a very well-trained Sha-

ron to act as Pat. That will be a good test to see if she can fool Steve that she is Pat!"

Mack replied, "Sounds good, I can leave this to you then and let me know if it works. Time is paramount in getting Sharon in Pat's position."

Mack then left and drove out the gate.

He drove to the house of Sir Ralph Walze and announced himself at the gate. He was admitted to drive up to the front door where he parked his car. He was then taken to the library where Sir Ralph was waiting for him. Sir

Ralph asked Mike to take a seat opposite him at the desk and then asked how the abduction had gone and what progress had been made. Mack told him it had gone well; a note had been sent to Steve's people and the test in the next two days with Steve and Sharon... as Pat.

Sir Ralph looked at him pleased and remarked, "what about Peter Morre?" Mack replied that he had told Peter that to keep him safe, he would only be informed on the bare facts, this being in his best interests. Sir Ralph laughed and said, "he doesn't know how much yet" and Mack smirked, nodding yes.

When Mack left half an hour later, he turned right at the gate towards the motorway. He passed a car parked in a lay-by and only gave it a quick glance as he could not see the driver. As soon as Mack had passed by, the driver who was bending down so as not to be seen, sat up and spoke into his radio informing on the car's number plate and that he had recognised the driver as Mack, who worked for Peter Morre. The voice on the radio said, "follow and keep with him, we will replace you at Sir Ralph's immediately, over."

The MI5 man started his car and sped off after Mack's car.

Mike was just about to walk out his office when his phone rang. He turned and answered it and was told by the operations operative about the phone call from the MI5 agent sighting, Mack, Peter Moore's henchman, and that he was told to follow him, and he is attempting to do so.

Mike answered, "good that is the right thing to do and we need to put a radio bulletin out asking the police and any agent to report sightings of the car, you have the car's number plate, so it should not be long before someone sees it.

Also tell the inspector on the Moore's case to get on it and try and trace where this Mack has been this morning and quickly, please."

Mike then rang Tony on his mobile and put him in the picture.

Tony said, "I think that Mack has something to do with Steve and Pat's abduction and maybe he has visited them where they are being held.

Mike answered, "That's what I think as well, I will keep in touch." He then cut off.

In the house where Steve and Pat were being held captive, the woman who was her captor and jailer, woke Pat up and told her to dress as she was going to be taken on a trip to meet someone who wanted to talk to her.

Her abductor stood in her room while she reluctantly dressed and then they both went downstairs to a car that was ready with the engine ticking over, and as they got in, it drove off at a fast pace.

Five minutes after they left, another car arrived and it seemed like Pat had returned, but in fact it was Sharon dressed and looking like a complete image of Pat. She was rushed through the door and was met by the butler person who took her to her room.

She sat at her dressing table and phoned Steve in his room. It took a while to get an answer and a very tired sounding voice finally answered and said, "Hello"

She answered, "Steve, I'm about ready to go down for breakfast, are you ready?"

He replied, "Sorry no, I've had a disturbed night and need to get a shower and dressed .... Do you want to go down or can you wait for 20 minutes?"

She replied, "I will go down and have a cup of tea and order our usual, ok?"

Steve looked at the phone as though he could not understand the reply! Pat going down on her own!! "Ok" he said and put the phone down, then sat for a few seconds thinking.

Pat's double left her room and went downstairs. She found where they had breakfast and then said to her female companion who was her 'go-for', "well that's the first contact over and it seemed to go well. Please order the usual breakfast. I will have a cup of tea and wait for him."

Steve arrived 20 minutes later like he said he would. He took a seat on the chair opposite her and very quickly their meal was put in front of them and they both began to eat.

As the meal went on, the conversation was very much about nothing important and Steve asked Pat if she had any incline from her captors if they had mentioned when they would be released? Her reply was, no not yet. So, he then said, "well Sharon must be getting fed up of waiting to take over and get started in your position by now." She looked a little bit annoyed and then composed herself by saying, "well, she can wait; I will not give in so quickly". Now he thought, that sounds more like Pat. His suspicion was still at an alert phase though.

He then asked her if she would like a walk in the garden after breakfast and she replied, "Yes, we could do, it would do us good to get some fresh air and sun."

They finished and both went into the garden together. They walked along to the end and they normally went to the right. He stopped, bent down to tie up his shoelace and left Pat to turn down the path they normally took.

However, she did not; she went down the left turn instead. This convinced Steve that she was not Pat, but Sharon on a try-out with him to see if they could fool him. They could fool most people but not him, he thought. He stood up thinking well; I will let them think she has fooled me. And then he thought, but what's happened to Pat?

The fake Pat had reached a bench and sat down before he caught up with her.

He sat beside her and said, "What do you think will happen to you when they are ready to replace Sharon in your place?"

It seemed to please her that he thought she was Pat, but she obviously had never considered what might happen to Pat, as the surprise showed on her face.

Steve made his mind up to do something tonight when they have retired to bed.

In the meantime,

he thought, I need time on my own to think and plan my next move. So, he turned to Pat's double and said, "do you mind spending some time on your own, as I need to have a nap as I did not have a very good night." She turned as they walked back along the path, "no I don't mind, I need to read a book and would be happy for a few hours doing so on my own." Steve nodded and they parted at Pat's room door.

Steve entered his room and went to the terrace door, which was open. He sat thinking with the scented air from the flowers drifting in.

Steve thought if he could somehow reach Mike that would be good as they could then organise a search for Pat. So, he thought... right, communications! Telephone, umm..... No chance of finding a mobile, have not even seen one!!

Then he decided that he would go again at night, at the same time, down to the room he had come through the previous night with all the equipment in. Failing this, he would have to escape. He then contemplated this possibility and concluded that if he escaped it could endanger Pat.

The room with all the electronic items in would be where he would need to start to cut off the alarm systems that could send warning signals of his escape when he climbed the wall.

This done, he went to his bed, flopped on it and slowly drifted off to sleep.

He was woken up by Pat's double with a cup of tea; it was nearly 6.30 pm, almost dinner time. He thanked Pat for waking him and for the tea. She smiled and left. He had a quick shower, got ready for dinner and walked down to the dining room.

CHAPTER 16

A Breakthrough

The Agent who was following Mack was in constant radio contact on his car with MI5 on the journey. He had caught up with Mack very soon after he had left the surveillance of Sir Ralph's house. They were now on a motorway and he could keep a reasonable distance behind Mack's car so that when he took the slip road to come off the motorway, it was easy to follow him on his next A road.

Several police cars came over the radio saying that they had sighting of both him and Mack and it looked like Mack was going into London.

Mike had the information relayed to him and was making sure they had several cars ready to follow Mack in London, by alternating the cars so Mack would never get suspicious that he was being followed.

Mack did not go into the middle of London but arrived at a small motel. The MI5 agent who had followed him stopped far enough not to be noticed but close enough from the reception desk to overhear what was said. He heard Mack ask for Chris Black. The receptionist rang the room and informed the occupant a Mack was asking to come to his room. The receptionist said to Mack, "room 100, on the first-floor sir." Mack nodded, went to the lift and waited.

The MI5 agent went very quickly up the stairs and waited where he could see the lift as it came to the first floor.

Mack came out the lift and went to room 100 and knocked. The door opened and a tall black-haired male opened the door and let Mack in.

Mack looked round the room and besides the male who was called Chris Black; there was also a female whom he didn't know and Pat Morre!!

Mack asked, "Chris, is everything running smoothly?" He got a nod that said yes. The female quickly took Pat into an adjoining room before Pat could see who it was. Chris mentioned to Mack that they were not taking any chances to let Pat see him. Mack replied that he appreciated his quick thinking and then he asked if they had everything they needed, to which Chris replied, "yes" and so, Mack then left.

The MI5 Agent had got back in his car to notify his control of the motel's address and that there appeared to be other people inside the room. He then quickly said, "Mack has come out and is walking to *his car, I will follow him. Suggest that Room 100 is visited very carefully, just in case the kidnapped subject is inside. Over.*

The control relayed his message to Mike who replied that the inspector and armed police were on the way. He informed them to be quiet and careful as their suspect victim may be inside. Control acknowledged and relayed the message to Inspector Dave Watt, who was now nearly at the motel. He relayed the order for no sirens and that no one should get too close.

Inspector Dave and his sergeant arrived first and parked around the corner near the motel. The police arrived and blocked all nearby roads, Armed police cars were in place. Four armed police then walked alongside the inspector. He had instructed them "no firing until ordered, unless it's to protect yourself or a colleague."

The Inspector went to the office where the reception was and told them that they were to arrest a person or persons, in Room 100. He was told by the manager that the cleaners were near the room, So the inspector got a plain clothed female officer to put on a coat that the cleaners wore and to push the cleaning trolley to the door. She was told to insist that the room towels needed changing and that she had two males helping her and that they were near the trolley.

She knocked on the door and it was opened by Chris Black who said, "yes, what do you want?" The police person replied, "need to change your towels, sir." Chris replied "ok, wait a minute" and nodded to the female to take Pat into the bedroom. He then allowed the cleaner to come through the door, but before he could close it, the two other cleaners pushed the door in. They covered his mouth, cuffed him and then searched the rooms and found Pat and her captor. Luckily, the female guarding Pat was looking out of the window to check if the cleaners were genuine, when the two police persons had entered the room.

She was cuffed and the room was filled with police, the Inspector and his sergeant taking over.

A message was sent over the radio that two people had been arrested, both had been armed and that Pat Morre was found in the hotel room. The message asked that MI5 be notified that she was ok and safe.

When Mike got this message, he let 'T' know. He was pleased they had found Pat so quickly but gave the order that this case must be kept secret so that Steve could be kept safe, until they find out why Pat alone had been kept in this motel room by the people who had abducted both Steve and her!

Mike now put into action his plan. He needed to find out why and who were connected with the abduction and if there were any links to terrorist activity or neo Nazi type organisations. Who were flexing their muscles in London and Nice?

He rang Nicola to put her in the picture and asked if she and Tony could sort out the French end and he would sort out the London end.

He had just put the phone down when it rang again. He lifted it, went silent a few moments and then said, "thank you, control"

She said, "the MI5 agent is still following Mack, who is going into central London." Mike replied, "tell him to stay with him; he has support following as well."

Mike turned to Jean who was in the office with him and asked her to go to the motel where the two kidnappers were and to check with the Inspector if there was a safe house where they could keep Pat. She smiled and said, "I'm off" and left.

The MI5 Agent following Mack realised that

Mack was heading towards central London. Mack parked in Peter Morre's office car park, then walked to the road and hailed a taxi. The agent notified his control and said he would follow the taxi into London.

The taxi took him to an area where there were a few gentlemen's clubs. Mack got out and walked into one of the clubs.

The MI5 agent contacted control and gave them the address. He asked if he should go in, but said he might be denied entry, as it looked like a private 'members only' venue, an officer's military club. After a short silence, Mike came on the radio and told the agent to not go in as he had just the person who could legitimately get into that club – him. He was a member of that club!

Mike rang 'T' who immediately replied that he would get an agent who he uses for these types of jobs. His name was George and that is all that Mike needed to know but he will report back to him. Mike smiled to himself; this was 'T's way of saying that George was not his real name!!

At the club door, Mack said he was a guest of Sir Ralph Walze. The reception told him to go to the lounge and that Ralph was expecting him.

A well-dressed older man then came to Mack and

said, "this way, sir." Mack followed and Sir Ralph turned round as Mack walked into the lounge. He was dressed in a navy suit and a military tie and said,

"welcome Mack, let's have a drink and a talk and then we will have lunch." Mack replied, "mine's a whisky" and sat down facing Sir Ralph, who beckoned a waiter to bring the drinks.

Then a man came into the lounge, walked over to Sir Ralph and said, "Ralph, good lord it's a long time since I last seen you! How about a drink and maybe after lunch, a talk?" Sir Ralph smiled and replied, "of course, George, I will make sure we do, old boy!"

George shook his hand, patted him on the back and then walked off.

George had very secretly pinned a small microphone to the back of Sir Ralph's coat and then went and sat nearby, pretending to read a newspaper. He had a fake earring aid in his ear so he could clearly hear Sir Ralph and Mack's conversation.

Sir Ralph was listening to Mack's run down of the kidnap of Steve and Pat and that both had been treated very well. He also gave him an idea of the training that Sharon, Pat's sister, had done and how she had excelled at it, but without doubt, she had a hatred of her father and Peter.

He concluded with explaining the way they had substituted Sharon for Pat at the house where she had been kept captive and that there were no indications from Steve that he was aware or suspicious of the swap.

Sir Ralph then explained to Mack that he had done right to keep Peter out of this as he had other ideas for him!

He went on to inform Mack that it was not just the shares that he was doing this for but with his group of followers, he intended to infiltrate the R&M group and even eventually take over its business and more importantly, the UK MOD contracts. It would make his group and associated groups very wealthy and powerful, so there was a lot at stake.

Mack looked astonished at him and commented that he hadn't realised those were his intentions and said, "Why shouldn't I have some of the gains that you will get, when it all works out?"

Sir Ralph laughed saying, "you will Mack. I look after those who look after me."

There is a group near the villa in Nice that are doing a lot of the planning; I have people all over Europe."

Ralph stood up and said, "Well, shall we eat now" and they both walked towards the dining area.

George had recorded the conversation. He then put it in a small box, sealed it and got the man at the reception to send it round to a business address he used who would send it on to MI5 and Mike.

He then finished his drink and went to lunch with a friend who had come to meet him.

Mike received the recording and immediately asked Inspector Dave Watt who was in charge of the kidnapping, the second in command of MI6 and 'T' to meet with him in his office.

CHAPTER 17

The Investigation

Steve played the recording to them and said, "This alters the meaning to Steve and Pat being abducted. It appears Sir Ralph has got more ideas on getting the shares and the R&M group for the future.

It would give his people a lot of finance and access to other businesses in the world. Even if he did not get the MOD contracts, he will have access to contacts and networks with people who do. This is a brilliant move if it came off. I would suggest that it's also is a terrorist threat to the UK and should be treated as such"

'T' said, "I agree, it puts a different perspective on this case, and we should treat it as two cases. One case is a kidnapping. The other is a terrorist case. I would recommend that the people stay on the kidnap one who is already working on it and with the terrorist side; we deal with it separately by using one of our specialist groups. It also brings in my friends from MI6."

The second in command of MI6 said, "Nicola, who is in Nice is one of our best on terrorists and can carry on with Tony who is knowledgeable on the R&M group case and the kidnapping. If she needs help, she will request it as she has a team of agents out there working with her

I suggest we make Mike the coordinator of the two groups and he has already sent Jean to look after the lady involved in a safe house."

Mike then said, "Yes, I agree we are set up ok at the moment, but I consider it imperative we locate and release Steve as fast as we can, before they realise what has happened to Pat and her two kidnappers."

While all this was going on, Steve was unaware of what had transpired in London.

He was carefully planning his escape via the control office at side of the house.

He planned to try and get out this way at approximately 10.30 pm, the same time he had passed the men last night. It will need luck, as they may decide not to go on a walk and have a cigarette tonight, but damn it, he had to try something. So, he settled down to wait his time and do the normal things he did in the day.

Mike was busy listening to a second recording that George had sent on the conversation that Sir Ralph and Mack had at their meal. He realised that in Sir Ralph's eyes this was his big chance to become the top person in his nationalistic groups in the UK.

Mike was now joined by Rob from MI6 whom he knew, as they had worked on a few cases together.

Mike turned the recording off and said, "I still think the sooner we get Steve to safety, the better. I just wish we knew the place where he is being held captive. The two we got in the Motel are not saying anything; they are professional killers and know if they speak, they're dead.

Steve was now having his evening meal and making small talk with Pat, alias Sharon.

She suddenly said that she did not feel well, and would he mind if she went to her room. He offered his sympathy. She stood up, walked very quickly out of the room and didn't even pick up her purse.

Steve thought it might have been an upset tummy. He picked up her purse and had a quick look inside. He found a mobile phone, so he put it in his pocket and put the purse back where she had left it.

A few minutes later, the butler person came in and asked, "Where is madam?"

Steve replied, "She left in a hurry and did not look well. Can you get someone to check on her please?" He nodded a yes and then went to her chair to put it under the table and found her purse saying, "I better let her have this as well." Steve looked at him and said, "I didn't see that, of course she may need it." The butler person left with the purse

Steve decided to go a walk in the garden although it was getting dark. He told the butler person who was going to clear the table that he would not be out very long, just getting fresh air. He turned the garden lights on which annoyed Steve, but he found a spot where he would not be seen from the house and with bated breath, he dialled Mike's number.

Mikes phone rang and he said, "Hello, Mike here!" Steve replied quickly "it's Steve. I've managed to get this phone, and no one knows that I have it. Is there some way you can trace my call?" Mike said, "keep talking and I will arrange a trace." Rob had got the gist of their conversation and had already rung through to the tracking department to do this. Mike replied, "if anyone comes, don't speak, but are you ok?" Steve replied yes and Rob then said, "Another minute and we will have the trace." Steve said very softly, "they are coming to find me."

Mike asked Rob, "have you got the trace?" and Rob replied, "wait, yes they have got it."

Mike said into his phone, "see you soon, take care, do nothing and cut off now."

He walked to the internal phone, dialled and then said, "I want the house surrounded now, silently, no one to go in or out until I arrive and tell our special squad, silence is the game." He and Rob then left in a car that had been ordered by Rob.

Steve casually walked back as the butler man was coming down the path. He had hidden the mobile phone in a small hole in the wall behind a shrub and said to the butler person, "hi, I was just coming back, it's getting chilly."

Another male came up, he was one of the security men Steve had previously sighted having a cigarette last night.

He stopped and said to Steve,

"Your lady friend seems to think that her mobile phone is missing!!"

Steve laughed and faced him, and then he commented, "do you mean Pat?" He said "yes?" "Oh" replied Steve," that's funny, she must be ill and it's affecting her mind. We both had our phones taken from us when we first came, so how could I get a phone that you already have?"

This annoyed the man partly because he had let the cat out of the bag that it might not be Pat!! And, because he knew Steve was challenging him.

The butler said, "let's get back, frisk him first" Steve stood facing the security man who frisked him and then said, "Nothing there, she must be dreaming it." They all walked back to the house.

Mike and Rob arrived and stopped a good few yards away from the house that had a high wall with wires on top indicating alarms. The steel gate had a camera and a speaker.

Mike got together the officer in charge and the officer leading the special armed squad. He gave them his plan of action and instructions.

The special squad with Inspector Dave Wall, his sergeant and other police would disconnect the camera and speaker and then go like hell in through the front way.

Rob and himself would go with some special squad officers over the back wall and enter that way. They were instructed "no shooting unless threatened, we don't want any casualties. Now let's move, you all have photos of Pat and Steve, so let's go."

Walking to the wall, Rob asked Mike if he was armed and he nodded yes.

Steve was sitting on his terrace just waiting, when he thought he had seen a slight movement near the top of the rear wall. Looking again, at the top of the wall, he thought, yes, it's those MI5 agents.

He had a torch. Everything around him was pitch black; no one was around, so he did a Morse code "S HERE, TO THE LEFT, PAT"

Mike saw this and using his torch, he replied "OK, UNDERSTOOD"

Mike and the others went over and within minutes they were inside through the back-bay doors.

They went through and the police, Mike and Rob went up the stairs.

Mike tapped Steve's door and Rob let himself with a policewoman into Pat's room

Steve chuckled and said to Mike, "well, it took you long enough!"

Mike smiled and said, "well, we have Pat and Jean's got her in a safe house."

We got the armed kidnappers who were with her and so I assume it is Sharon who is next door?" Steve said, "Good job."

"Mike, let's get away from here, I've got a small bag with my tablets in, let's go."

When they got outside Steve noticed a police car driving off with Sharon inside with a police-woman at the side of her.

Steve and Mike got in Mike's police car and it drove out of the front gates. They were followed by the other cars, all going on a 30-minute drive to the New Scotland Yard building in London.

AN UNFORGETTABLE MEMORY

Part 3

CHAPTER 18

The Case Develops

Mike had Steve dropped off at his hotel. Steve was instructed to shower and change, then get his breakfast, but to contact no one until Mike had arranged with him his next stage in the Morre case. He was also told to pack as he would be going to a safe place as soon as it was arranged.
He was told to ring Mike when he was ready to go to his office and be de-briefed.
Mike also arranged agents to make sure he was protected and never in a position of being approached by anyone that could put him in danger again at the hotel.

Back at MI5, Mike rang Jean who was his wife and an agent of MI5. He put her in the picture of Steve's release and the dangerous position he had been in. Mike mentioned that they also had Sharon, Pat's sister, and that there was to be no communications between Pat and Steve, but Pat could be informed that Steve was ok. Jean could also tell Pat that her sister, Sharon, was in custody at this moment. Jean thanked Mike and told him to be careful, wished him well and then they rang off.

Inspector Dave Wall had sent a message that the two kidnappers were not talking and were obvious professionals. He also informed Mike there were a lot of papers to go through that may provide results.

Mike rang 'T's' PA and arranged a meeting for later in the morning.

He then contacted Tony in Nice, to tell him Steve was ok, but he and Nicola must now get the terrorist and Nazi connotations sorted by working with the French Secret Service and the CIA, who also had interests in the case. He finished the call and sent a note to the second in command of MI6.

Mike sat a moment digesting in his mind his moves so far, he then rang Steve in his hotel. Steve answered and Mike asked if he had been for breakfast.

Steve replied, "no, I'm just about to finish dressing, sort my packing and then go to the dining room."

Mike said, "Steve, in half an hour, I will be going to the canteen for breakfast. I would like to meet you there so we can talk while we eat. Could you be there, please? Remember the password is

IVANHOE, mention this if anyone asks who you are and they should answer, SAXON. See you in half an hour then."

Steve sat in the reception area waiting for the car to arrive not realising two MI5 agents were also nearby, in case of problems.
The car driver came in and asked at the reception for Steve. The receptionist pointed to Steve, who was sitting in one of the armchairs with a case at the side.
The driver walked over to him, asked if he was Steve Long and he replied. "No, Ivanhoe." The driver smiled, put his hand out to shake Steve's hand and replied "Saxon." Steve shook his hand and they both got into the car.
The agents followed in their car.

Mike was waiting in the dining room and was ready to order when Steve arrived. They both ordered an English breakfast and toast. Mike smiled and said, "You haven't lost the habit of the usual breakfast we always had on our missions."
Steve shook is head in a no and then when their meal came, he briefed Mike on what had happened at the house and on how his captors had made a mistake of expecting Sharon to fool him.

Eventually, they got to discussing how Mike had to sort out the Morre case, which included Steve working with MI5.

Steve agreed for Tony to be co-opted to MI5 temporarily and to work with Nicola on the Nazi doctoring mixed in with terrorist activists in Nice for as long as it took.

Mike said to Steve, "I have to keep you safe although I want you to investigate the Morre case, so you will be staying at a safe house and be protected by agents. You will only use transport that we provide, and it will be driven by an agent."

Steve replied, "I understand, but I would like my female operator, Diane, to join me on the case as I know how good she is on picking up items that many people miss." Mike agreed.

Steve said, "I will ring her when I get a phone. I will ask her to contact you, to get her passes, etc. and that she will need to come stay at the safe house that I will be at". Mike replied, "that's fine and I will start to get things organised, may be good to use her to interview the two Morre's sisters, Pat and Sharon." Steve nodded, yes!

Mike then said, "You will have to hurry as you only have 15 minutes to contact Diane, before we go to a meeting with 'T.'

They then went to Mike's office and Steve was given a mobile phone. He rang Diane and explained that she be would joining them. She was very interested in taking it on and arranged to get to MI5 offices at noon with a suitcase packed and ready.

Steve sat at a computer and typed a brief report of his abduction, what had happened and his release by the police and MI5. He got Mike's PA to print the report and distribute it to all the people who were going to attend the meeting with 'T.'

Mike and Steve walked to 'T's' office, went in, and said hello to all who were there. This included the second in command MI6, a police commissioner introduced as Paul, an army officer of the rank of general, Steve, Mike, and the minister whose remit was the secret services.

Mike began by asking if they had received and read Steve's report? All nodded yes. He then went on to point out that the case of abduction was a criminal offence and would eventually be treated as such. He mentioned Inspector Dave Wall was leading on the police side and he would eventually deal with the abduction side. Except at the moment, it was being kept to only certain people knowing about it until investigations finish and the tie up with the organisations abroad are investigated, and he hoped would be brought to justice. He mentioned that he also had a team led by Nicola and Tony investigating this and he intended to have a team in the UK, led by Steve and his assistant, Diane, to investigate the R&M group and where the connection was between them and the Nazi /Terrorist connections and why.

'T' asked Steve if he had anything to add. Steve commented that he was still puzzled himself why the nationalist group abroad was interested in the R&M group and in particular, Pat.

The second in command of MI6 said he would support them in any way they needed it. The Police Commissioner said the same and the General commented he had specialist military units ready if needed. The Minister with no name said, "it sounds as though you have the resources to sort this and you have my backing."

'T' ended the meeting and Steve and Mike left to go back to Mike's office. Mike gave Steve a pass, a mobile and a tracker and wished him luck. Steve went to the front entrance to meet Diane

She was pleased to see Steve and gave him a hug. Steve had organised their car to take them to the safe house to settle in.

Again, they were unaware of the two MI5 agents that were following them.

The house in a London suburb was a good size and had a wall and grounds and the usual security gadgets about.

Steve and Diane spent an hour discussing the case and he briefed her on the picture so far.

Diane said she would like to spend time with Sharon and talk to her as she is in London still and at New Scotland Yard. Steve arranged this but informed Diane that she would have to do this on her own, as he felt he must rest and sleep as his illness was catching up with him.

The car came to take her, and Rob a MI6 agent got out and introduced himself. He explained that he would go there and back with her to make sure she got all the help she needed and that both she and Steve were not allowed to go anywhere without an agent protecting them.

On the way, Rob talked about working with Steve, Ray, Tony, and Mike. He told her that he knew they were all together in the commandos and so were very close comrades.

He told her that Steve was older than the others and had left the Regiment a few years before they did, but they kept in touch.

Rob said that he had worked on several cases with Mike and Ray. He had got to know them well and like the comradeship developed in the Forces, it was part of their comradeship now, so he had a special reason to help them as well.

Diane was very interested in this and like Rob, she was pleased to be part of Steve's team and with Tony as well. She had been in the Forces and was also police trained.

They arrived and Rob took her to a part of the

interrogation area set out like a lounge and she sat on an armchair, while Rob brought Sharon in with her female police escort.

Diane introduced herself and explained that she was on the case with Steve.
She gently got Sharon to talk by being a friend she could lean on who understood how men could treat women.
Sharon explained how she had fallen for the wrong man and no matter who had told her she would be let down and treated badly with the man she had chosen, she was in love and so took no notice of other peoples opinions, including her father's.
She was told by Josh Rodriquez to go and that he had threatened to cut off the allowance he had given her.
Eventually the man left her, and she ended up having to go to any sleeping place she could find. She used drugs and was sleeping rough, but she would not contact her father or sister to ask for their help.

Eventually, she met another man called strangely, Robert. She fell for him and he persuaded her to get back with her father and he took her to the villa near Nice in France
The people there tutored her and explained everything that they wanted her to do. She was a

quick learner and was transformed into her sister, Pat.

They then sent her to the house they had Steve in, saying if she passed the test of fooling Steve, she would be rich and if she did as they said, she would also be safe!

However, when she left the villa to come to the UK, she found out that Robert had disappeared. So once again, she had been duped and left to face the consequences on her own!

Diane thanked her and said, "You are among people now who do their duty but have no intention of making you the scape goat in this case. I advise you to cooperate and a meeting will be arranged for you to see your sister soon."

Diane thanked her and then Sharon left with the female police officer who had come with her. The entire interview had been recorded and would be distributed only to the people who need to be informed.

Rob of MI6 had watched and listened to the interview and on the way back in the car to London, he mentioned that he thought Sharon was only a pawn and used by the abductors and who would have got rid of her after they had got what they wanted. Diane intimated that she thought Sharon wanted to be helped particularly with her drug problem and that Pat when informed of this, would help her sister to go back to a normal lifestyle. By this time, they arrived back at New Scotland Yard.

CHAPTER 19

The Terrorism Investigation

Tony and Nicola had contacted some of the people she used as contacts for information. In this case, those that had Nazi ideals and terrorist actions.

One of them was Jewish trader who had come into contact with a new organisation and who was now dominating all the other small groups. He was aware that the leader of that group had amalgamated all the smaller groups of them into a formidable larger group. He did not have names nor know the leader, but he knew of them.

Nicola reported this to her people and to the French Secret Service through Carl.

They were disturbed by this information and were doing more investigations.

Also, two Israeli agents had joined Tony and Nicola and these agents were doing their own investigations, which they normally do when notified of any Nazi ideals in existence.

They were concentrating on the villa first to get information on people involved and would share their findings with MI5 and the French security.

Tony and Nicola arranged to go to a gambling casino together, to see what they could find about the organization that the Jewish man had mentioned was being formed.

Tony was in a dinner suit and Nicola wore a long, beautiful grey dress with jewellery glittering at her throat. Tony thought she looked stunning and outshone every other woman in the place.

They sat at the roulette wheel, steadily winning until it got to the point that other people noted their success and began to follow their betting.

So did the casino's management and the owner decided to meet them.

The manager offered to introduce them to his boss in the back office. Tony squeezed Nicola's hand and they both accepted the invitation.

They were escorted upstairs to the owner's office.

Entering the room, they saw at one end was a desk with a telephone and behind it, a wall full of TV screens showing different parts of the building. There was also a man monitoring the screens.

On the left of the desk, was a chair come bed, where the owner sat reclined with two, lovely young ladies next to him.

Ahmed the owner had a bunch of grapes in his right hand and the girls were giggling whilst picking grapes and feeding him.

Ahmed was a big man all over and as far as most people knew, he was of Arab descent.

He was known to be the man who in Nice who knew everything that was going on.

He spoke to Nicola in a very high voice for a man of his bulk, "err, my beautiful friend from Britain, I believe you have been asking questions about a new organisation based on ideals the Israelis dislike intensely.

Now you come to my place, why?"

Nicola playing along said, "Thanks for the compliment, but I know you well enough to be sure, that you of all people would be aware of this," and smiled at him, which he showed, he liked.

"My friend, Nicola," he said, "I will tell you that you are looking in the wrong place. They only have minions in Nice! Their meeting place is in Texas, America.

I will also warn you that they are ruthless and dangerous, and this is as much, my beauty, I will give you. Would you and your friend like a drink?"

Nicola said, "Ahmed, my pardon, this is my friend, Tony, and thank you for your offer and advice, but we must get on. I will meet you again some time, no doubt."

He bowed his head and they left and as they walked down the stairs, Tony said, "Do you believe him?" Nicola gave a quick laugh and said, "Yes I do. Shall we go back to HQ and report? We then can go for a meal."

Tony nodded yes and she took her phone out of her purse, spoke into it, and walked with Tony to the entrance doors.

Within a minute their car arrived, and they went back to their local HQ.

Mike at MI5 received the report from Nicola and sat thinking for a few minutes. Then he picked up the phone and rang a number not even 'T' was aware of

A voice answered and Mike said, "thank goodness, I got you Brad. I have some information that you may be interested in!"

Luckily for Mike, he had contacted Brad who was a CIA agent who went through a lot of US and UK missions in cooperation, when they were in the forces and since he became a CIA agent.

Also, since then he had worked with Ray and Mike on the code name Golden Eagle case to a successful end.

Mike gave him a rundown of the present case he was working on including the information just given on the kidnapping and the findings at the villa in Nice. Plus, the Ahmed information, on the unnamed new group of terrorists now being formed.

Brad replied, "Sounds like it's just the type of mission for me. Let me have words and I will come back with a suggestion to put to 'T'.

Hope you're keeping ok Mike" and then he cut off.

Mike sat back thinking if we get the CIA on our side, that will help a lot in the USA.

Tony and Nicola having made their report were then taken by car to a very nice little restaurant.

They were on a table set back from the main ones, giving them a good view of the rest of the diners. They both noticed a table of 6 people, all couples dressed very well and no doubt enjoying themselves.

Nicola looked at Tony and said, "I guess we have hit the jackpot. Those people are the three people and their wives who I want to have words with.

Maybe we can just be up front and ask them what we need to know."

Tony asked, "look at the table behind us, with those three men on.

Are they bodyguards?"

"Sort off, but worse," replied Nicola.

"That's a bad idea then" said, Tony.

"Yes, I think so," commented Nicola.

Tony took a bite of his steak and said, "it's a pity to spoil a good meal"

Nicola laughed and before she had a bite of her steak she said, "I'm going to the ladies, I'm taking my purse and I will phone Carl."

Tony nodded yes and continued eating.

Nicola got up, went to the restroom and was back in 5 minutes. She sat down and in between bites of food, she informed Tony she had made the call and they were on their way.

Carl had got together some of his special police squad together with four Israeli agents and set off to the restaurant.

On arrival, he got the leaders of each group together and informed them they were to get the bodyguards first as they came out to get the cars, and then they were to get the three couples when they came out to get into their cars. All were to be taken to the local police HQ for interrogation.

He then went into the restaurant's reception and gave the waiter an envelope to give Nicola.

This informed her of the plans to capture the three people they need to interrogate and where they would be taken.

Nicola and Tony sat talking, waiting for the couples to finish their meals. Their drivers had left and about five minutes later, the couples left. Tony and Nicola followed and observed the police taking them into custody and then followed them to the police HQ.

They observed the interrogation and noted that the people accused were too frightened to give any information about the new group being formed in the USA. Although, unknowingly they had provided some pointers, as to where the group was based, and it was a group that was aiming for world dominance.

This was mainly gained by the Israelis giving them questions that were scarier than the fear that they had of the new organisation.

Tony and Nicola both went to the MI5 HQ. They reported this to their sections and waited for a reply.

The reply from Mike was quick. He informed them that tomorrow they would be told by the CIA in Texas, America, that the CIA would be investigating the organisation. The message would come from Brad, who knew Tony. Brad would make sure they had all the support they needed whilst in Texas.

They did as they were told and on awakening the next day, Tony received an early phone call from Mike, who did not seem to have slept well. Tony informed him there would be no need after all to go to Texas as Brad had found out that the leader and some of his main people were going to be visiting Nice, and that they had rented a 19th century villa for the week along the road from the main town in Nice. They are would be hosting a large conference with visitors from many different countries attending, including Sir Ralph from the UK.

The French Secret Service had been notified and Nicola and Tony would need to work with them.

Nicola had already received a call from Carl requesting ta meeting that morning with Tony and herself to discuss their plan of action.

CHAPTER 20

Another Problem

In London, Steve was with Diane and Rob of MI6, they were in a car going to a place that was used by the police for interviews and security of the people to be interviewed not known to them at all due to not wanting the people they were after getting to know, in this case Pat and Jean from MI5, her companion.

It was a big mansion on the outskirts of London and as they drove through the gates, Steve noticed an armed guard as they passed by.

They rang the doorbell, showed their ID passes and were taken to a library type of room with bookshelves, desks, chairs and a slight smell of mustiness. Steve thought this place was not used a lot.

Sitting on a settee, surrounded by big easy chairs at one side of the room, was Pat and Jean.

The three of them sat in the easy chairs saying hello and some small talk.

Steve started by asking if Pat was ok particularly after her kidnapping experience and she replied, "yes fine, thank you but Sharon has been let down again by a loved one and is semi dependent on drugs."

He then continued to tell them both about the visit that Diane, his assistant, and Rob from MI6 had with Sharon. He said their impressions of her present state were not good.

However, the plan was to get to the bottom of why Steve and Pat had been abducted and the method of the kidnapping. Steve mentioned that he did not think it was to get Pat's shares but a way of having the R&M group in their control, although they were not yet sure of identity of the person directing the take over and why!

Pat interjected by saying, "I will see that Sharon is taken care of and receives appropriate treatment for her drug problem. I will also make sure she is ok for finance and try to get her eventually back on track with her living standards."

Steve smiled at her and replied, "I know you will look after Sharon even if you have to deal with your father's views about her."
She shrugged her shoulders and said, "Don't worry about him; I will get him to accept it."

"Good for you" Steve said and continued with, "Pat. I'm afraid we have to keep you in a safe house until the case is sorted but if you feel you would like to see your sister, it can be arranged." Steve then laughingly commented, "I think that will do for this meeting, I can smell the coffee coming". They all giggled and started to talk to each other casually.

Steve and Pat walked to the patio windows, looked out of them, and admired the scenery. Pat asked Steve if he was ok and whether he had got hurt during the escape.
He looked into her eyes and replied, "no, not at all but I was exhausted and had to rest but I'm ok." They smiled at each other and Steve squeezed her hand.

While Steve and Pat were talking in London,

Peter Morre was in his office and discussing with Mack how he thought the kidnapping and replacement of Pat was going to work.
Mack was not aware that Pat had been rescued, she was free and that the two kidnappers were in custody.
He gave Peter an update on when he had seen Pat and kidnappers at the motel and Steve in the house near London. He told Peter that Steve was unaware that it was Sharon and not Pat that he was with.

Peter asked, "Did you know that my villa that they had stayed at in Nice, France, had been raided by the police? It is closed as the search is going on and the staff is in custody whilst charges are being considered."

Mack was shocked and said, "No, I didn't know that, but there's nothing the police can do about my people staying there!"

Peter's face went red and in a loud voice, he said, " no they cannot, if they have found certain items inside the place, then that's a problem and they will get them to make certain accusations on his nationalistic connections!"

Mack went silent and let Peter carry on. Peter was now shouting and blurted out that he had found this out from his contact, who like himself, was not happy about the trouble this could bring.

Mack quietly said, "can I phone someone from here and check something out?"

"Press the button on the phone near you and ring the number" was the reply.

Mack said, "Bill, is that you? It's Mack. Has anything happened at your house with the visitors?"

He went silent listening to what Bill was saying and then after a minute, he put the phone down. He had gone very white in the face.

He looked at Peter and slowly said the police had also raided the house where the two people were being held, so this meant that Sharon was now in custody and the house was being searched.

Mack thought Peter would blow his top, but surprisingly Peter calmly said, "well, it looks like your idea has been a disaster. Whose house was it?"

"It was Sir Ralph's!"

Peter stiffened saying, "I think you had better disappear for a while as he will be furious and will want a scape goat to take the rap. It is a calamity and like the issues at my villa, it's going to take a lot of time and money to sort."

Mack hurriedly left the office, got into his car, and started it but before he drove off, he rang Sir Ralph and briefed him
on what had just happened in Peter's office.

"When did this all happen? "asked, Sir Ralph.

"Yesterday apparently" replied Mack.

Sir Ralph sighed "I wonder why I've not been informed or are MI5 waiting for a reaction from me?

Mack go abroad whilst I sort out things at my end. Put everything on hold"

"Will do" replied Mack, who then

put his phone in his pocket, revved the car and put his foot down as he drove out the gate of Peter's office car park

A car with two MI5 agents then followed him reporting to their control that they were doing so.

Mack went straight to his flat in London and in his bedroom, he hurriedly packed a suitcase.
He rang a contact who he knew would help him to arrange a private plane that could take him to France in the afternoon.
He took some cash and other things he needed from his safe and then set off for the private plane's aerodrome, which was an hour away from London. He checked in at an office and was then taken by a stewardess to the waiting lounge. There was about an hour before the flight took off, so he ordered a whisky and then sat back for the wait.

The car with the agents in parked unseen at the aerodrome and one of the agents walked to the office to enquire if they did business flights.
He then returned to the car, got on radio to control, and asked them what his next move should be. He had found out that a plane would be leaving in less than an hour to France, landing at a private airport not far from Nice and that Mack would be on it.

Mike replied on the control radio and told him to

get on the plane, he would find the flight plan and which airport they would be landing and that agents would be waiting to follow him over there. Within 15 minutes Mike rang Tony and informed him that Mack was on his way, told him the name of the airport and asked that he follow him. Nicola had all the details about Mack sent to her and the airport he would be landing at.

Mack was quite content to be taken by the stewardess to his seat on the plane, it was very luxurious inside and there were plenty of drinks.
So, he sat back to enjoy the flight quite smug that he had got away very easily.
Mack left the plane with the stewardess's address that she would be staying at and had arranged a dinner date with her that evening.

He picked up his luggage and then got a taxi to the large villa where he was attending a conference at the weekend. He sat back in his seat feeling contented that he was going to have a nice weekend and a dinner with a pretty lady. He had got out of the UK before he could be questioned by the police and looking out the car windows, the weather was sunny.

The taxi was followed by Tony and Nicola who were in an agency car and their driver knew the roads and area.
He told them that it looked like Mack was heading

for the large villa that was rented by an organisation the British Secret Service and French Secret Service had an interest in.

They arrived and stopped discreetly, hiding the car in a wood near the villa.

Tony and Nicola had a look around the wall and gate and decided it was alarmed and well protected by electronic alarms. They went back to the car and arranged for surveillance on the place and left when this came, instructing the agent to inform them if Mack moved and gave him a photo of Mack.

Mack paid the taxi; he then rang the bell and a butler answered the door. Mack said who he was and that had rung previously to arrange his early arrival.

He was taken to a row of one-story flats and given the first one.

He thanked the butler and did a quick check for any bugs. He did not find any, so he sat down with a cup of tea and started planning his evening.

CHAPTER 21

The Mystery Needs Sorting

In London, Steve had arranged to meet with Diane, Jean of MI5, Sharon, and Pat. Sharon and Pat greeted each other very nicely as sisters and Sharon became very relaxed and talkative with Pat
They were not aware that they were being recorded by the authorities.

Steve took a back seat and said little as it was very much a joining of sisterly love, after so long.
They found out that a man named Mack had organised the abduction of Pat and Steve, he was the front man and had organised the kidnapers to do the job.

Sharon only knew about her role in the process and apart from Mack, she and had no knowledge of the other organisers.
This was helpful but they got no indication what the long-term purpose was if Sharon had succeeded in impersonating Pat.

After this meeting, Steve met with Mike and said he was not happy as he could not find a reason why they tried to get Pat's shares in the way that they had done as it could have been done easily by agreement later. Something didn't add up!

Mike agreed that there must be a good reason for the risks that were taken and said, "I feel it in my bones that there is a connection with the organisation we are now investigating. We need information on the conference and a list of attendees. I have certain agents working on this."

Steve commented, "I think Sir Ralph and Peter Morre will have covered their tracks and with the lawyers that they can afford, they will state that they had no idea on what was happening!"
Mike agreed and said, "that's why I'm leaving them in the dark on what we know but keeping an eye on them. As a matter of fact, I'm talking to someone recommended by MI6, this afternoon. Would you like to attend with me?" "Yes, I would" was Steve's quick answer.

They arrived at the meeting place in the MI5 building and were shown to a room set out like a comfortable lounge with a settee, armchairs, small tables nearby and a bar in the corner. They sat on the settee. To their left, was the second in command of MI6, 'T' and a General.

There were small round tables with paper and pens on and everyone was offered drinks

'T' said, "we have got the paperwork on the man and woman as they work well together. Both are incidentally qualified and experienced, so could make a twosome." He then asked for them to be called to the meeting.

The male was about 6 foot and looked very fit. He was well dressed in a dark navy suit and tie and had an air of authority about him

He was a major in the paratroop regiment and well trained in the skills required to work on MI6 missions. He spoke fluent German and French and had been on several undercover missions for the secret service.

His real name was not given, he was to be known as Zach Dupree. He was the son of a German officer who served in WW2 and immigrated to the UK after the war.

The story for his cover was he took up where is father left off as an officer of Third Reich. Zach had joined the British forces but continued his contact with an organisation with Nationalist Socialist Doctoring (NSD).

The Female was a trained MI6 agent. Her real name was also not given, she was to be known Sophie Dupree, Zach's wife. She could speak fluent German, French, and Spanish and like her husband, she also had an interest in the same organisation.

She was medium height, had black hair down to her shoulders, wore a suit that fitted her all in the right places and had a beautiful, smiling face that could charm any male.

The most important reason for them attending the meeting was the organisation leaders and wives would be attending the conference in the French Nice area.

They had an invitation and would attend the conference as man and wife. MI6 would instruct them on their mission and provide their contacts, etc.

Also, the code word was "Ivanhoe" and the reply, "Saxon"

Mike and Steve now had access to the inner part of the conference.

They both thought the kidnapping and the switching of Sharon for Pat had to be part of a bigger picture involving a new amalgamation of nationalistic groups involved at the conference.

Mike and Steve had kept the kidnapping and the capture of the others a close secret so that Peter Morre or Sir Ralph would be free to go to the conference. They could then be followed and arrested at the right time as and when necessary, ready for any eventualities that may arise.

Tony and Nicola had found out that Mack had arranged a date for dinner. They knew at which restaurant and booked a table themselves at same place.
They dressed for the occasion and were now travelling to the restaurant, fully prepared for any eventuality.
They were given a table which was a little way back from the dance floor; it was a good position to observe all the other tables.
They ordered their meal.

Mack had given himself plenty of time to arrive for his date with the stewardess and being early, he sat in the entrance foyer to wait for her.
When she walked in the door, he gave a gasp at how lovely she looked in evening dress.
He greeted her with a peck on the cheek and they went into the restaurant. Mack as he always did, a quick scan of the other diners, and was satisfied that they were harmless.
They both sat down unknowingly at a table that was directly in front of in Tony's vision. Tony also had the ability to lip read when he needed too.

The evening went on and Nicola and Tony enjoyed their meal and wine.
Tony commented that Mack and his date seemed to

be enjoying each other's company.

Soon the band struck up and like other couples, including Tony and Nicola, Mack and his date went onto the dance floor.
They all danced to several tunes and near the end of a waltz, Nicola tripped and bumped into Mack's date.
Nicola thanked Mack's date for helping her to a chair and as she sat down, she said, "hi, I'm Nicola" and the reply was, "hi, I'm Kath" and they both giggled.
Tony spoke to Mack and apologised for Nicola bumping into his date and blamed the highly polished, dance floor.
Mack casually said, "No worries, it happens" and they all started to talk and ended up in the bar to enjoy a drink.
When it came time to depart, they arranged to meet the next day at a café and to have a walk around the Riviera. But Nicola and Tony said that they would need to check their work diaries to see if they could have some time off and asked Mac and Kath not to wait for them if they were late.

Tony and Nicola were driven to the headquarters in Nice where they emailed their reports to Mike at the MI5 building in London.
They had both agreed that they didn't think they would get any useful information from Mack and that Kath was just his date and it was not likely

that she would know anything about his connection to an organisation named SOOWN. However, they would keep an agent to tail them.

Mack took Kath back to her hotel, they kissed and agreed to meet the next day at the place Nicola and Tony had mentioned.
When he returned to his villa flat, he emailed Peter to let him know where he was and texted Sir Ralph's special number to inform him of his flat number in the villa.

He sat on his chair thinking about Kath. He really liked her, but she would be back on her plane tomorrow afternoon and it would be some time before they could meet again, after their second date tomorrow.
Well he thought, "I've beat the UK police, I may as well enjoy my date with Kath tomorrow and then get back to business in the evening."
He then went bed and got sleep very quickly.

In the MI5 building in London, Steve and Mike sat discussing the situation. Steve told Mike that Jean, Diane, and Rob were in a meeting with Pat and Sharon. They were all in a room that was bugged and had a two-way mirror for observation. It was hoped that Pat and Sharon would be able to shed light on why Pat had been kidnapped and Sharon's role in the matter.
Mike commented that they had let Peter and Sir

Ralph attend the conference in France and that Mack was under surveillance, and so hopefully this would be additional sources of information.

Mike received the reports and informed Jean and Steve about their contents.

It was good that Tony and Nicola had contacted Mack, but the main item was the meeting with an American man, whose name was Bill Wilde.

Brad through the CIA had informed Mike, that Bill was a very rich man and seemed to be the head of the new organisation, called Special Organisation of World Nationalists (SOOWN)

It was believed that Bill had a SOOWN agency with a leader in every country and they reported directly to him.

If they failed badly, they would not be seen again anywhere!

Steve was still confused with the connection with the R&M Group.

Mike was sure their people at the conference in the French Villa would be able to make the link.

They both agreed to continue the path they had taken to solve this but to instruct Diane and Jean to push Sharon to make her speak, as time was not on their side.

Steve played the recording of Pat and Sharon's meeting again. Something at the back of his mind now made him feel very suspicious of the sisters. He came to a part of the conversation where Sharon asked Pat, "do you still keep in contact with Joe, your ex?" and Pat replied, "no way" and Sharon said, "oh, I thought I spotted you about 2 weeks ago in a hotel in London. I was having lunch in their restaurant, but I kept well back as I didn't want you to see me." Pat gave a giggle saying, "no sorry, it wasn't me." Sharon gave her a puzzled look and said, "Oh, guess I was wrong."

Steve played it that part of the tape again. He then rang Diane and told her about the conversation between Pat and Sharon. He asked Diane to check out Pat's movements, where she had been and who she had met up with in the two weeks before he had met Pat on holiday. Diane agreed and asked, "do you want warts and all?" Steve replied, "yes, everything. Not sure what but something is niggling me!" Diane replied, "ok Steve, leave it with me" and cut off.

CHAPTER 22

The Day of the Conference

The MI6 Agents, Zach, and Sophie were on the flight to the conference. They arrived on Saturday and had an invite to dinner that evening.

Zach's face had been altered with a moustache, glasses and greying hair and he was dressed in a well-fitting suit and tie. Sophie had dyed her hair red; she had a lot of makeup on and wore a very expensive looking suit.

They were both relaxed and sipped on gin and tonics. A car would be waiting for them at the airport and after they arrived, they would have just enough time to unpack and get dressed for dinner.

They had the information about the conference and the organisation they needed to give them a good cover and Zach had already been approached by telephone by Bill Wild, the leader of the organisation to sit near to him at dinner!

They were met at the airport by Tony and Nicola, who briefed them on their end of the case and on Mack's movements. They were also given their phone number to use if they need to.

Mike dropped the two agents off at the villa and left saying, "you know where we can be contacted, good luck."

When they arrived, the receptionist gave Zach a note from Sir Ralph. The note was an invitation for pre-dinner drinks. Zach accepted.

When they were in the flat that had been allocated to them for the weekend, Zach said to Sophie, "we don't have not a lot of time to change for the evening, looks like we are very much in demand, so just take care and let's watch each other's backs." He then blew her a kiss. They commenced to shower and get ready.

Back in London, Steve was sitting finishing his dinner, it was a bit late, but he needed food. Mike came in with Jean and as they sat down, he said, "I would have thought you would be in bed catching up on your sleep Steve. You look exhausted."

Steve looked at him and with a cheeky smile said, "not too long ago we all could stand this pace but now I'm not as fit and healthy as I was then. I'm ok thanks, nice to see you both."

Jean smiled and said, "don't overdo it Steve. Please do as you are told."

Steve then explained what he had found on the recorded meeting with Pat and Sharon and what he had asked Diane to investigate. Jean replied, "perhaps we have something" and she made a phone call to find out.

Mike looked at Steve and said, "what do you think is going on Steve? I know you don't do anything without having a notion of what you are looking for?"

"Well, I think there is much more to the taking over of shares by Pat and she have an accomplice to help her. I know she has a good business head but so have Peter and Josh, so how come she beat them to do it? If I am right, then I may have been led up the garden path like a fool and I do not take kindly to that," replied Steve.

"Well, I know," remarked Mike.

Jean said, "we will find something, I'm sure of it and I will inform you as soon as I get it. In the meantime, I will question Pat a bit more and try and get a reaction that may give us a lead. I will also get Diane to question Sharon Morre. She may know more than what she has been saying to us."

In Nice, Zach and Sophie arrived at Sir Ralphs pre-drinks event.

It was very busy and there was not a lot of room, but despite this Sir Ralph, his wife, Peter Morre and his female escort were quickly at their side, offering them drinks and arranging to take them to a side room to meet Bill Wilde, his wife and their friends.

They were escorted by a lady who was well versed in various languages and introductions were given as they walked past people of different nationalities. Eventually they got to Bill Wilde, a tall very well-built man dressed in a well-tailored dinner suit. He looked and spoke like a man who was used to being obeyed and not argued with and he had a Texas drawl in his voice. When they were introduced to Bill and his wife, Bill's face changed to a nice smile and a pleasant voice tone. He shook hands with them, welcomed them to his conference and informed them that he would be interested in hearing more about their organisation and its size, during dinner.

Zach and Sophie walked over near to the door, having picked up a glass of champagne each. Zach said to Sophie, "Bill is treating us like royalty! I guess he must want our organization in his plans." Sophie smiled and in a very low tone of voice replied, "he gives me the creeps. I felt he was stripping me with his eyes" Squeezing her hand, Zach replied "hold it Sophie, I understand but that's the problem with men like him in powerful positions. I'm 6 feet 2 inches, he must be 6 feet 6inches. Among this crowd, he has power and the money to make people do what he wants them to do. We must play along but it would not hurt if you stayed aloof and ignored any intentions if he shows them. I will do the same and show him that we will not be forced to do anything, just because of his power and money."

Sophie smiled and nodded, yes. Suddenly a voice of a male came from just outside the door informing them to take their seats, and that they please look at the table layout on the notice boards near the door entrance.

They joined the crowed going to the dining room but before they had got very far, a lady who had been fussing around Bill came up to them and said, "please follow me, I will show you to your seats." So, they did.

They were sat opposite each other at the corner of the table nearest to Bill, his wife and his second in command and his wife.

When everyone was seated, Bill stood up and amidst much clapping and cheering around him, he gave a toast to his SOOWN organisation and its subsidiaries.

The dinner then began, and several toasts followed the first course and all the courses after.

Sophie and Zach heard about the SOOWN organisation from different people. They got the impression that almost all the conference attendees were involved in the ideals of the socialistic, Neo Nazi doctrines of this organisation. Apparently, the organisation was becoming worldwide and had many training areas for their swelling army of troops in some countries.

It was also forming large industrial conglomerates that were very rich and powerful, indicating an intention for it to be a force to be reckoned with. Undercover terrorism would be used to attack vulnerable governments and take over economies that were not viable, with the aim eventually to produce their own currency.

After the meal, certain sections of people were invited for drinks. Zach noticed that Mack and Peter were not included but Sir Ralph was.

Most of them had partaken in wine drinking quite liberally, they were near to being completely intoxicated and were given notes!

Sophie found out the next day that those people would have to present reports for their areas to the top members in the main echelon of the organisation.

Zach and Sophie had also received and accepted an invite to be on the balcony to observe the presentations. There were to start at 10.15 am the following morning.

They also found out that there was a ban on using phones on the next day starting from midnight, this evening. Zach and Sophie agreed a coded message would go from their phones before then to a MI5 special number, informing them of what they had found out. In case the conference organisers were monitoring mobile signals,

Sophie went to the ladies' room, drafted a message very quickly but did not send it until they were walking back to their flat in the open air. When she had done this, she gave her phone to Zach, who took out the sim card, put it in his pocket and then stamped on the phone. It would now not be recognisable. On the way to the flat, he found a paper bag in a waste bin, he put the pieces in it (without the sim-card) and placed the bag back in the waste bin.

In the flat, he burned the sim and disposed of it in the rubbish bin. They still had his phone if they needed one as they were potential board members.

On the way back in the open, Zach commented on the night and their findings and that it looked like they had been accepted as aspiring top board members.

Sophie agreed but said, "Zach, I think we should get some sleep so that we are ready to face everything tomorrow." She then kissed his cheek and went into her room.

Zach was just sitting thinking; he then stood up and walked into his room.

Tony and Nicola had been out for dinner and walked hand in hand through reception in their hotel, when the receptionist handed Nicola an envelope. She opened it and said to Tony, "we have to ring HQ."

They went to Nicola's room and she rang the number and was soon put through to Mike. He informed her that the two agents inside the conference had been invited to observe the higher echelon board meeting. Also, that Mack and Peter had not been invited, but Sir Ralph was. He told them "be prepared to support them at a minute's notice, if needed." Mike then cut off.

Tony commented that it seemed like the agents had been accepted by Bill Wilde and other people in his company!

They alerted everyone they needed to, including Carl of the French Secret Service and the CIA.

CHAPTER 23

The New UK Branch!

Zach and Sophie had their breakfast and as they made their way to the board meeting, they came across people from all over the world, including China. Before they had left their apartment, they set up traps in their apartment on suitcases and drawers by using their hair in some cases, which would be dislodged or broken, if tampered with.

As they got to the large room where the meeting was to be held, the lady who seemed to do all Bills bidding approached them and guided them up the stairs to a small balcony that took 6 people.

They sat where they were told to and found they had a good view of the square long table which had place names and folders on each chair space. The table soon filled up with a very diverse group of people such as Chinese, American, Arabs, African, French, German and many more, making it an international attendance.

Everyone went silent when Bill Wilde took the chair at the head of the table. He started the meeting by asking participants to provide a verbal report on each of their areas.

China had a good report on expansion, as did the USA, Middle East, and Russia, but lagging was the UK.

Sophie held Zach's hand and squeezed it to let him know this 'lagging' was reason why they had been invited to attend and to give them an introduction to the work and vastness of the organisation.

Then the full truth of Bill's leadership came into view when he received a report from East Europe. He told them in a bitter voice he would not contemplate failure and then asked the rep to leave the meeting. A woman stood up, she looked very frightened and was escorted out of the room by two bodyguards. Zach and Sophie assumed that they would never see her again.

Their impression of Bill was that without a doubt he was a maniac, like Hitler in the past wanting world dominance and was he was brainwashing people to believe in it that.

The meeting finished and Zach noticed that Bill's bodyguards had come back and escorted him out of the room.

A lady that had met them previously when they had arrived, came up to them and started fussing around them. She offered to arrange a meeting for them with

Bill in ten minutes in his office.

Sophie and Zach walked down to the small café, they ordered cups of tea and sat in the corner to discuss whether it would be a good idea to meet Bill.

Sophie started of with, "Zach; we would need to be very careful. Bill is used to getting his way and it could be dangerous for us if he does not get what he wants."

A waitress came along with two cups of tea. She smiled as she placed them on their table and casually asked "are you Mr IVANHOE?" Zach smiled at her and replied "SAXON." She smiled back and replied, "Contact made, I can pass any information on, if needed." And then she walked away.

Zach said to Sophie, "we now can pass on our info of this morning's meeting." Sophie smiled back and said, "I think I had better do my visit to the lady's room." She got up, took her handbag, and left.

On her return, she said she had done a quick update note and when the waitress came over to clear the table, she slipped it to her.

The time had come for them to meet Bill and the lady was back fussing around them whilst ushering them into Bill's office.

The room looked like a library and had a desk, a phone, chairs, and a settee near by the desk

Bill was sitting behind the desk puffing on a cigar and his two bodyguards were sitting on either side of him.

Zach thought to himself, "no way of getting at him here then!"

Bill spoke to them in his Texas drawl and informed them that he wanted them to lead the UK branch of SOOWN, this being the highest office he could offer them as he knew that they could do the job.

They would have full control on their own budget and would report directly to him.

Sophie said, "thank you Bill but we need some time to think on your offer as neither of us do anything by half. Also, we need to think about and discuss the other plans we already have.".

Bill grinned, looked at Zach and said, "Lucky man." Zach smirked back.

Bill's smile then faded, and he told them that he expected an answer before they left the conference today. Then he immediately dismissed them.

Zach and Sophie returned to their flat but on the way back they stopped to sit on a bench where there was no one around them and to have a talk.

Zach started off by explaining to Sophie that taking up Bill's offer would mean a complete emersion of themselves in the organisation for it to look that they were genuine. And if they failed, then they knew what the consequences would be as they had only just observed what had happened to that lady at the Board meeting.

He continued to say that not only would it be a dan-

gerous mission, but it would also be very difficult to keep in close contact with Special branch agencies.

To Zach's surprise, Sophie agreed with him and was willing to take the risk, as she put it, "this is what I was trained to do."

Zach then commented that if they refused the offer then they could be killed to keep this all this quiet. He then got very agitated and said, "I don't take kindly to being put in this position either. Let's do a note and give it the waitress and ask her to pass it on."

Having done this, they arranged to see Bill and went back within 15 minutes to his office.

Bill was pleased and informed them to get their end sorted as soon as possible because within a week a very important person from an Arab royal family was going to be visiting the UK. He explained that SOOWN would be issuing a contract to eliminate him and when this was done, his country would be in a mess and one of SOOWN Arab members would then take over that country with help from the UK branch of SOOWN.

The organisation would be using Sir Ralph to pave the way diplomatically and make arrangements for a welcome dinner, where Mack would carry out the elimination.

Zach and Sophie came out of Bill's meeting very annoyed they had fallen into his trap and were now in collusion to this act.

They went back to their flat, packed and waited for their car that was soon outside the entrance. It was a Daimler saloon
Soon after they set off, Zach opened the sliding window to allow him to speak to Tony and said, "Will your mike stretch to the window?" Tony stretched as far as he could to the window and Zach then asked, "Can you get me Nicola please!"

It crackled and Nicola came on saying "I have earphones on, only the operator and I can hear. Over" He then informed her of the elimination and the role Bill had asked him and Sophie to play, which altered everything they had previously discussed.
Nicola replied, "Carry on planned, I will get back to you after speaking to 'T'."
Zach handed the mike over and sat back saying to Sophie, "we have to wait now for 'T' to decide whether we carry on or disappear. If we disappear that will leave Bill puzzled?"

Steve was in London and had made enquiries about Pat and Sharon but found nothing that would concern him. He was relieved about that. Pat had seen her ex-husband a few times, but it was only a quick meeting which indicated that he might have been trying to regain some of her shares.

So, after talking to Mike, they decided that they

should concentrate on Peter Morre and Josh Rodriguez in the hope that it would uncover a reason as to why they had carried out the kidnapping.

They had also by this time decided that Josh was not in anyway a danger to the girls except as a very strict father who wanted to have his own way and was not very kind to Sharon, after she had left home in the past.

Having also had the chance to talk to the ladies separately, Steve was convinced they were not involved in the kidnapping, any more than Sharon being duped by Mack's people to get her own back on her father.

After receiving reports from the conference and now being aware of the elimination, Mike and Steve decided to concentrate their minds and energy on Peter, his son Joe, Mack, and Sir Ralph.

They also agreed that no arrests would be made but to keep a 24/7 check on all their movements.

After leaving the villa in France, Mack went to a place near Paris where he knew of a contact that could organise eliminations but at a price.

He arrived at a shop that sold books and asked for Jacque. A lady went through the rear door and returned saying, "Please go through, he is at the back."

Mack found Jacque, they shook hands and Jacque said, "Long time since I met you. Are you ok?" Mack replied, "Yes I am, thank you. I have some business to offer you if you have someone who can do the job."

He then briefed him on the Arab Prince who he wished to dispose of and the place where it could happen.

Jacque knew the person and the place. Also, he was aware of the SOOWN organisation. He sat a few seconds thinking, then said, "I have the perfect person who is a resident in the UK. I will get him to contact you later today. The price is one million pounds, half to be paid before the job and other half on conclusion. You pay it into my account, you have the details.

I will arrange for this man to contact you and after that, there will be no contact between you and I."

Mack shook his hand and then left to get back to London by the private plane he had arrived on. He had no idea that he was being followed by Tony and Nicola, who were responsible to keep him in their sight as far as possible.

The shop Mack had just left was one that the French authorities were keeping an eye on because of the suspicious people who visited it.

Nearby, Tony was standing looking in a shop window when Mack came out and was walking back to his car. Tony noticed that a female started to casually follow him. Tony had seen her earlier near the shop and there was no doubt that she was tailing him.

Mack walked to the car park, got into his car, and drove to the private airport not realising that he now had two cars tailing him.

Nicola had found out by radio, that the female was a French Secret Service agent. She was to be informed that they were also following Mack.

It was decided by Mike in London and the French Secret Service, that the female agent would take the same flight as Mack.

Tony and Nicola would leave from Nice airport as they had people who would be waiting where Mack would land, near London.

Tony was keen to return to the UK and get after Mack, who he knew had been involved in Steve's kidnapping.

He was also pleased that he and Nicola were still working together.

Mike, Steve, and Jean were in the MI5 building in London.

They were in the canteen going through all the evidence they had on the case. They knew the R&M group with Pat, they knew that Peter and Mack were involved in the shares and kidnapping and they now knew of the connections to the socialistic, Nazi organisation, called SOOWN and the elimination that was being organised.

They had agreed for Tony and Nicola to focus on the kidnapping, the role that Mack had and the elimination. Rob of MI6 would be on standby to support them if needed.

Diane and Steve would concentrate on Peter and Pat and the shares.

They were also aware that all the different parts would eventually tie in together at some point and that they would be ready to deal with it when they got to that stage.

CHAPTER 24

A Chase on the Elimination

Mack had arrived back at the same airport near London on the private airline he had left on. He also had a chance to re-start his romance with the stewardess as they were to have dinner the next evening.

He hailed a taxi at the airport to take him to his flat in an exclusive part of London, where one or two MPs also lived.

He had a quick sandwich and a coffee, then showered, changed, and set off in his car which he had left in his garage nearby.

He had received a telephone message from Jacque to meet a contact at Hyde Park at a given bench in a certain position near an entrance where he usually parked.

He got to the park and walked to the bench. There was a medium sized, grey haired man with glasses already sitting there. He had a small dog on a lead and was wearing a raincoat, gloves and was smoking on a pipe.

Mack sat down on the bench next to him and said,

"It's a lovely evening." The man answered, "Not for late summer." Mack then relaxed as it was the reply that Jacque said the contact would make.

The man then turned, patted his dog, and said, "I have all the info and will be here, Sunday at 12 noon."
Mack smiled and replied, "I have finished with my newspaper, would you like it?" The man nodded yes so
Mack gave him the newspaper and then stood up and walked back to his car.

The French agent who was following Mack had photographed this meeting and after Mack had left to go to his car, she continued to follow him.
When she got back to her car, she radioed through on the MI5 band to her control and reported what she had witnessed.
Steve heard her message and asked her to come in with her photos, etc. as a couple of other agents were now following Mack.

Tony and Nicola started their car and followed Mack's car as he left the Hyde Park area bound for his office in central London.
On the way, they received instructions from Mike to follow Mack wherever he went and to report back at regular intervals as he suspected that the man Mack had just met, might be the eliminator. The grey-

haired man was also going to be followed. He and the dog had left the park and were on a bus to the East End of London. He got off at his bus stop and whilst walking to a small flat in a multi-storey block, he acknowledged several hellos and shouts of "hi Bill." He took the lift to the second floor, walked to his flat and went in.

He put some water in the dog's bowl and then sat down near his phone and dialled Jacques.

When his call was answered, he said, "I've accepted the job and received the first half of the money. I will let you know when the job is done." He then put the phone down, walked into his bedroom and took off his disguise. The face in the mirror was the face of Joe Morre!

Outside, the MI5 agent was sitting in his car watching the flat.

It had started to rain and he gave a deep sigh and was just about to pour a cup of tea from his flask, when he saw Joe Morre, who he recognised from reports he had read, leave the block of flats. So, he quickly contacted control and informed them.

A reply came back asking whether Joe was going by taxi or a bus and the agent replied, "Neither, by underground, he has just started to go down the steps to it."

Mike replied, "Follow him. I will get someone in a minute or two to cover your present position."

The agent quickly locked his door and ran after Joe.

Luckily when he got to the underground, he saw that Joe was in a long queue buying a paper. He reported this on his mobile phone to control.

He had no trouble getting a ticket for his destination and was only two people behind Joe in the ticket queue.

The agent who sitting outside the grey haired man's block of flats was just settling into his waiting mode when a knock came on the window and Steve got in the car, explaining he heard the radio messages and he had come to investigate the flat occupied by their suspect. He told the agent to stay outside in case the grey-haired man does a runner.

Diane then came to the car and Steve got out and they both went in through the front entrance door. They took the lift to the second floor and found flat number 20.

They knocked the door and got no reply, nor did they hear any dog barking, but they did from next door, number 22.

Diane knocked on that and a lady holding a dog opened the door and Diane said, "hi, I'm Diane I am trying to see your next-door neighbour, but I'm getting no answer. The lady said "no dear, you won't as he has just left, and I look after his dog" "Does he go out a lot then?"

"Yes, dear he does, and we have an arrangement

that I will look after his dog and keep an eye on his place."

"Do you think you could show us the patch in his bathroom ceiling, please? He reported it to his landlord and the landlord has asked us to look at it."

"Sure dear, no problem. I will get his keys and we can take a look."

She then smiled, said her name was Doris and went into her flat fetch the keys.

When she returned, Diane introduced Steve to Doris. He showed her one of the many false ID cards that he carried on him, this one being an inspector of property!

They three of them went into the flat and Steve headed to the bathroom and other rooms to check for damp patches.

Doris stood in the doorway with Diane and explained how the man who she said was named Bill, rented the flat and spent a lot of time away on business. She was happy to look after his dog and his flat.

Steve then appeared and he and Diane thanked Doris for her help and said the landlord would write to Bill to arrange for the repair. They then said goodbye and as they walked to the lifts, Steve said to Diane, "There is a lot more to Joe Morre than we know. I think he is the eliminator that we are looking for." As they drove away, they waved goodbye to the agent.

Steve rang Mike at the MI5 building and re-counted to him what had happened, and that in his opinion, Joe Morre was the eliminator hired by Mack to murder the Arab Prince.

Mike agreed it seemed so, but they need strong evidence before an arrest could be made. He asked Steve to stay on the case with Diane and that he would arrange with the agents to make sure Joe does not get away from them until he incriminates himself, so they can arrest him

Steve confirmed this was ok and said, "has the agent tailing Joe Morre come back with where he went after leaving his flat?"

Mike replied, "Joe has gone back to Peter Morre's office and the agent is waiting for him to come out."

Steve then said in reply, "right I'm going to Peter's office to just upset them both and see if we get a reaction?" "Ok," said Mike.

Diane had heard the conversation, so she drove the shortest route to Peter's office.

Steve told her, "they will probably try to use their positions to overbear us but I intend to shock them a bit to see if they will get angry and drop anything out that we can then use to detain them."

When they got to Peter's office, the PA recognised Steve and when he asked if Diane and he could see Peter, she contacted Peter on her intercom and he replied, "certainly, send them in."

She opened Peter's door and as they walked in, they saw Joe seated in front of the Peter's desk. Joe pulled up two chairs to the right of him for Steve and Diane. Steve introduced Diane as his colleague.

Peter very nicely said to Steve, "welcome. Are you here for any particular reason?".

"Yes, I am very interested in your connection to the SOOWN organisation and why?"

Peter had a Havana cigar in his hand; he put it in his mouth and puffed. He looked at Joe then back to Steve. He went very red in the face and replied, "why is that anything to do with you?"

"Answer the question and I will tell you!! Or have you something to hide by not saying anything?"

Peter scowled and he menacingly said to Steve, "people can get in real trouble asking those sorts of questions!"

"What trouble, may I ask? And as my client is dealing with you and the ombudsman, it is my duty to protect both in the share deals and in any take over of other businesses involved."

Peter sat stuttering, "go to hell, go to hell!!"

"I will take that as a yes then," grunted Steve.

Joe then interjected with, "what specifically do you want to know?"

Steve replied "this organisation has links to certain other organisations with Nazi beliefs and terrorist intentions towards the UK and the crown. So how can you trade as a company with a branch of MOD contracts? I think the Board should ask you to resign from being a director of this group and then you can then get involved with the SOOWN organisation as long as you are willing to face the consequences of being named a traitor and terrorist."

He then told Joe the same applied to him as he obviously did what Peter told him to do and continued with, "you will also lose the income you are used to Joe, unless of course you do other jobs to swell your income?"

Joe looked very sheepish and said, "I repeat what my father said, you can get into a lot of trouble saying these sorts of things!"

Steve replied, "Is that a threat from you both?" "You figure it out" said Joe.

With this Steve and Diane stood up and left the office. As they drove off, Steve rang Mike and told him of the meeting they just had with Peter and Joe and that Diane and he would now need bodyguards 24/7.

Mike replied, "you certainly have put him in a position of now taking action. I can see why you did it. I think he may try to get rid of you both and it will be difficult to legally prove it. Steve you do like to live dangerously!!"

Steve replied, "as you well know Mike, sitting back waiting for them to give us evidence could take time which we have not got, so now he has to act in some way. I also think Joe is the eliminator and should be followed so that we can get information to arrest him,"

Mike replied, "Already arranged. I don't suppose you spotted Tony and Nicola waiting to tail Mack who was in the building as well?"
"No, you have me there," he replied.
"Well they reported seeing you come out. Over".

Steve looked at Diane, "I'm afraid you're stuck with me for a while."
She smiled and said, "Story of my life! I will manage."

After Steve and Diane had left, Peter immediately rang Mack and said, "I need to see you right away!!" He then put the phone down and looking, directly at Joe, scowling, he said, "we have to shut this man up, he can do us too much damage in many ways"

As Joe nodded a yes, Mack knocked on the door and Peter shouted, "come" Mack walked in and sat down in front of Peter's desk.

Peter began by saying, "I've just had a visit from Steve and his colleague.

He is threatening to discredit me plus other things. I want him stopped.

I don't care how you do it, but I want no connection to me or Joe."

Mack looked at Peter, saying, "it will be done and sorted." He then stood up and left the office

Peter sat back in his chair and smiling he said to Joe, "he will sort it."

Tony and Nicola followed Mack as he drove by them and then reported it on their radio.

They soon realised Mack was in a rush to get to his destination and was overtaking cars at any chance he got making it difficult for them to keep him in view.

They ended up in an area that was not very well kept and was known as a thief's den.

Mack parked and went into a building that looked like it was long overdue for demolition. He made his way to an office area where the people he wanted to meet were having a drink and a get together to decide on their day's activities. This was mainly forcing local shops, etc, to pay an amount of cash for daily protection from other gangs who lived on this income.

Mack was welcomed by the apparent leader of the group.

They listened to his proposition and their leader asked Mack how much would be paid to carry out 'the accident.' Mack replied,

"£100,000 on completion of the job". The leader's face looked like he had found a money nest egg and commented, "What time scale, Mack?" and the reply was "as quick as you can organise something successfully, without any come back to you and me."

Then then all sat closer and discussed who it was and all the loose ends that would need tying up.

CHAPTER 25

It Starts to Unfold

Meanwhile as all this was going on, Tony was on the radio to Mike at MI5.

He reported where they were and that in his opinion, Mack was getting the necessary cut throats to eliminate Steve and Diane.

Mike said, "I want you and Nicola to detain Mack as he leaves or before he gets to his next destination. We need him out of the picture as we know his connections to SOOWN and the eliminator.

I will get agents to you within a minute. They deal with and know the thugs he would use, and they will let them incriminate themselves before we detain them.

This leaves Joe Morre who will try to do his contract on eliminating the Arab Prince at the weekend. So again, we must keep him on a short lead until we have the evidence.

The SOOWN organisation is being sorted by UK, US, and French agents."

Tony agreed and said, "Roger. Nicola and I will deal with Mack's detention with pleasure. I owe him one for Steve. Over."

Nicola looked at Tony and asked whether they should get back up and go into the place that Mack was in now or should they wait until he got to his next destination?

Tony replied, "as much as I want to confront him, I think we should wait until he gets somewhere that would be easy to corner him and where he will not have any help. Let's leave these thugs in there to the other agents and we follow Mack."

Nicola smiled and said, "See we can work together in the future." They both grinned at each other.

Steve had heard all this and was with Diane who driving when Mike and Tony finished on the radio. He put his mobile phone to his ear and waited a few seconds and then said into it, "Tony, can you let me know when you and Nicola go to apprehend Mack please?" Tony replied "sure boss, Nicola and I will let you know. Are you ok and keeping well?"

"Yes, and I'm ready for Mack." Diane smiled to herself knowing those two together were something to be very weary off.

Ten minutes later Mack was driving on the M25 and Tony and Nicola were following him.

They made sure he did not realise this and at one point they even overtook him in the outside lane, tucked in behind a car on the nearside lane, letting him overtake and then kept behind him. He suddenly started to drive onto the inside lane to get off at the next junction.

They continued to follow him, and he then turned off at the roundabout as though he was going to the airport but then he exited the road heading towards a rural area. He stopped at a motel along this road and parked. They followed and parked.

Mack went to a room not far from the reception office and knocked on the door. It was opened by the air hostess who he had met on his plane to Nice.

He stepped in.

Tony rang Steve and reported their position and said this might be a good place to apprehend Mack.

Steve agreed and had joined the M25 when Tony notified which road he was on.

Nicola had done a walk around the hotel room and found out that there was no rear exit so the only way in and out of the room was through the front door

Nicola had watched an older male go to the door with towels and within a few minutes, he went in and in 5 minutes he came out and went further along with his basket of towels. He was followed by the air hostess to the office and they both went in.

Inside the office, they pulled the old man out of his basket. Mack gave him his coat back and thanked him with a wad of money.

Mack watched another car turn in and park near to Tony's car. He smiled to himself as he recognised Steve when he got out of the car.

Tony, Nicola, and Steve went to the airhostess's room, knocked on the door and waited.

Whilst this was going on, a taxi drew up near the office and hid by the office door that had been opened by the old man, Mack and the air hostess got into the taxi. No one had seen them, and the taxi sped off.

The old man then returned to the office closing the door behind him. Nicola went up to him, showed her MI6 pass and asked if he had a key to open the hotel room.

The old man stuttered under his breath to himself about police, trouble and wasted time, these comments were just distinguishable. He walked with them to the door and opened it. Steve, Tony, and Diane burst in through the door with Nicola following with the old man. They went through the room saying 'clear' and it soon became obvious that Mack had cottoned on to being followed and had done a getaway, leaving them all with egg on their faces and embarrassed.

Tony dashed back to the car and sent out a message that if Mack was spotted, they must notify Tony and then apprehend Mack.

Nicola was concentrating on the old man who ran the motel, knowing he must have had a hand in helping Mack and the stewardess to get away.

After pressure was put on him, the old man talked and gave them the name of the cab company.

Very soon they found the cab driver who told them that he had dropped the couple to an underground subway near Peckham.

Steve was driving towards Peckham with Diane and said, "Mack knows how to lose himself in London. We now need a lucky break!!"

Diane smiled and replied, "the name of the game, Steve as you know!!"

He smiled back and Diane looked at him and remarked, "you look ill, Steve. I think you are overdoing it and have not had a lot of sleep. You have your best people on this case. Let's get back so you can rest. Tony and Nicola can cope." He looked at her very white in his face and nodded a yes.

Diane then radioed that she was returning to the

headquarters as Steve was not feeling well. Mike came on quickly telling Diane to take him to a private hospital not too far from headquarters. She could leave him there; they would take good care of him and she was to make her way back quickly to Tony and Nicola. He told her that he had just been informed by the terrorist department that their agents who had been following the gang who were going to harm Steve and herself were in a hotel in the East End and Mack had just turned up there. Mike had given the order to apprehend them all.

Steve heard this and in a weak voice said, "Go for it, Diane." And so, she put her foot down on the accelerator.

At the hotel in the East End of London all the roads were quiet and had little traffic.

Special Branch had surrounded the hotel nearby very discreetly

Tony drew his car up near a black van. Nicola and he then went into the van, which was in effect, a mobile headquarters.

It was occupied by police officers all very busy on screens and radios.

A chief inspector brought them up to speed on the position in the hotel. The suspects including Mack were in a side room having a meal and the only entrance into the hotel was guarded by armed police. The wall facing the car park was under observation by a special squad in case they tried to get away either through the door or the windows. Everyone in the hotel had been put in a safe area and the staff was now police constables, a male and female.

The group had just finished their meal and were waiting for the drinks they had ordered.

Inspector Dave Wall and his sergeant were coordinating the mission as they had worked on the case for a while and were very experienced in making arrests of this type.

Tony looked at the Chief Inspector and said, "I think we should go in and secure Mack whilst Special Branch deals with the others; ok?" The Chief Inspector nodded a yes.

Nicola had given Tony a gun and Diane had been armed by Mike from MI5.

Diane came into the van saying Steve was exhausted but in good hands.

She got a quick debrief from Nicola and they found the Inspector who agreed that they could be the waitresses. So properly attired, they set off with two police who were dressed as waiters, to take in the drinks that had been ordered.

The police led the way and the trolley was pushed by Mike. They went into the room which was smoky and full of noise. The gang were celebrating their windfall of money which had been paid by Mack to eliminate Steve and Diane.

Tony who was dressed as a waiter with a moustache parked the drinks trolley near to the gang leader and Mack. The waiters began to distribute the drinks to each one reading from a list saying their names out loud. The gang leader stood up while this was being done and when they all had drinks, he said, "let's drink to Mack and to the success in our coming venture."

Mack smiling was drinking his whisky when he suddenly felt steel on back of his neck and a voice behind him said, "you are all under arrest for attempted abduction and murder". At the same time, Nicola had a gun on the gang leader's neck. Diane was at her side.

The door then burst open and armed police swarmed in.

The gang members sat there looking shocked and it was Mack who said to Tony, "you won't get away with this for long!!"

Tony said through gritted teeth, "watch me and don't make a wrong move, my trigger finger needs some exercise!"

Mack knew he meant it and dropped his shoulders, looking worried. He turned and said to Tony, "have I seen you somewhere before?"

"Only in your nightmares," Tony replied. He pulled Mack to the door and together with Nicola,

Diane and two armed police; they took him to a black van which then took him off to be interrogated.

Tony turned to Diane and asked, "Diane how is Steve? "

"He's ok but needs rest and sleep to get him back on his feet."

Nicola said, "Well give him our best wishes when you see him." Diane nodded a yes, then went over to the inspector and got into discussion with him.

Nicola led the way back to the car, saying to Tony, "what do you think we should tackle next." He squeezed her hand and said, "I'm going to suggest we tackle Joe Morre!"

They turned the corner to get back to their car and all a sudden, they found Mike walking alongside them. Smiling, he said, "I've seen Steve's doctor. He will be ok; just needs rest and I've put Diane as his bodyguard.

They will tackle Pat with the shareholding and with all that's happened, we expect Peter's resignation and some of his shares bought off him.

He will now be held as an accomplice to the kidnapping and attempted murder. His lawyer no doubt would argue for leniency but he is finished in the business world.

Now that leaves Joe. I want you, Nicola, to deal

with him and sort out the role he played.

MI6 has given you full authority to deal with it."

Then grinning at Tony, he said, "and of course, Tony, we would be grateful if you would continue to help Nicola and in turn us on this."

Tony took the que and quickly replied, "I would like to continue on this."

"Good, that's that then" said Steve as he dropped back. They turned round to see him, but he had gone! Nicola and Tony grinned and shook their heads.

CHAPTER 26

The Eliminator's Chase

Nicola and Tony had contacted the agents tailing Joe Morre and they had been keeping a distance from him so as not to give him any idea that he was under surveillance.

However, this very morning he had set of in his car eastward and they somehow had lost him and assumed he had realised he was being followed. A full bulleting to report any sighting of him was circulated to all the patrol cars, rail police and transport people, including the buses in the UK.

So now all Tony and Nicola could do was wait. Tony rang Diane who was visiting Steve and Pat today to see if she would ask if either of them had any idea where he would be heading.

Joe had realised he may be tailed so to lose them; he did a sudden change of journey and direction.

He was an expert at keeping himself free of being tailed since he had become an assassin and so far, he was successful at it.

Joe was still driving eastward on the M11 motorway

and making good time. To anyone passing by he was a person on a break heading towards Norfolk.

He stopped after a while at a café and had a snack, a drink and bought a bottle of water to drink on his journey.

He had decided to go to his small cabin which was near an area he owned set in woods on the Norfolk coast and on private land. He paid a warden to keep it that way and to keep his estate in good condition, Here he could make his plans for the contract he had for eliminating the Arab Prince who was visiting the UK at the weekend.

Joe had studied the Prince's itinerary and the places he would be travelling too. He knew that it would be difficult to try to eliminate him on his journey or in his hotel as he would always be closely guarded.

He eventually concluded that the Prince had a friend who was a council leader in an area near his cabin.

He would use a sniper's rifle in a position near where the Prince and the council leader were going to meet to open a plaque to commemorate a well-known architect who had built the council offices.

Joe felt very content, he had lost his tail and had decided on his place to execute the Prince.

On his arrival, he rang several people that he dealt with and made arrangements to see one of them the following day.

He also decided to spend the evening with a lady friend he had known for many years and arranged for them to go out in the evening for a meal at a nearby restaurant.

Back in London, Diane had an idea that if she got Steve, who was now more or less back to his old self, to speak to Pat on the phone and explain what they know about Joe and his connections as an eliminator, maybe she would have an idea where he went to on the East coast.

Steve agreed and was in the process of having the phone conversation with Pat. She was very kind and asked if he was taking care of himself.

They then got to the point where he informed her of the evidence they had on Joe's secret. He asked if it meant anything to her and that Special Branch wanted to find out all they could about him to stop another death. She understood completely and replied, "I do know he has a cabin on a small estate in Norfolk and it's in the region of where Lord Nelson had a house somewhere nearby."

Diane had enough information, so she silently left the room, letting Steve continue his conversation with Pat.

Diane went to her car and rang Mike. He answered very quickly, and she updated him of her idea and on what Pat had said to Steve.

Mike said, "I will put all our resources on finding the cabin and I want you, Tony and Nicola to go to that area in Norfolk now! I will ring Tony and you three must find Joe and stop him from assassinating the Arab Prince. No holding back."

Diane drove to her hotel and packed, she was ready for Tony to contact her.

Within an hour Tony, Nicola and Diane were driving to the east coast to the Burnham Thorpe area of Norfolk which was known as the birthplace of Lord Nelson.

They were aware that the security service was already investigating the actual place that Joe Morre had somewhere in that area.

On the way, Mike informed them they had found the cabin's vicinity and they were to stop at a small wayside café near the area in question where they would be met by a local person who works for MI5 and who would guide them to Joe's cabin to reconnoitre it.

An hour later they arrived at the roadside café. They went in and found a table. Tony went to the counter and ordered toast and tea. While he waited, a tall grey-haired man with a walking cane came up and said, "hello, are you here to see Ivanhoe at the cinema?"

Tony said, "no it's too Saxon for me." They then shook hands and Tony guided him to their table

The tall grey-haired man introduced himself as Bill Stokes and said he lived nearby.

He did know Joe's cabin and said that it was well fenced by a high wall and that a game keeper, as he liked to be called, lived with his wife near the gate entrance. Also, that the cabin was surrounded by a thick wooded area and gave the cabin complete isolation, which was apparently what Joe wanted when he occupied it.

Nicola said, "well I don't think we need to get in the cabin, but it would be good to see the layout of the grounds."

Diane commented, "yes I agree, but we must not be seen. We don't want to give him any reason to get away again"

Tony said, "could we drive by and park close by near an area where we would not be seen?"

Bill smiled, saying, "yes, I know a place!"

Tony commented to the ladies, "I think there is more to Bill than meets the eye!!"

They then set off in the car and as they approached the entrance to the estate, Bill told Nicola to slow down. They had a view of the road to the cabin and the small lodge the game keeper lived in. Bill told Nicola to keep going to the next junction and turn left and then about 50 meters along the road, to turn into a path in the trees just far enough not to be seen from the road, then park. She did this and then Tony, Nicola and Bill got out, leaving Diane in the car ready to go at a minute's notice.

Bill took the lead and guided them to the wall that surrounded the wooded estate. They turned right along the outside until they came to a tree with branches grown over the top of the wall which if climbed, a person could drop over the other side of the wall.

Tony said to Bill and Nicola, "I'm going over to survey the area near the cabin in case we have to tackle Joe in there."

Nicola and Bill nodded yes and watched him climb up the tree along a stout branch and drop over the wall.

Tony dropped to the ground. He put two bruches off the ground in a cross near the base of the tree and he set off slowly navigating his way towards the cabin.

He went very quietly through the underbrush until he heard a shot.

He stopped and surveyed the area around him Crouching down, he heard a familiar sound of a rifle bolt being used not far away to his right.

He crawled a few metres and came across a man with a sniper's rifle about 7 metres away. He was at the side of a large tree with the rifle resting on a small branch to hold it steady. Taking careful aim, he shot at one of the melons dangling down from a branch of a tree quite a good distance away.

The bolt clicks, a few seconds to aim, then a shot, and like his last one, a splattered melon.

All Tony could see was a head with black hair and a sniper's rifle with a silencer on.

In his mind, he gauged the distance and crawled away thinking, "now I know he intends to shoot the Prince from a distance."

Tony climbed up the tree where he had left the crossed small braches and dropped down onto the other side near Bill and Nicola. They all returned to the car.

Tony told them what he had seen and was certain now that Joe was going to shoot the Arab prince and so they need to survey the area where the council's presentation ceremony was to be held. Then reconnoitre the surrounding buildings to see if they could locate a place that Joe might use to shoot from.

Diane then asked Nicola and Tony, "if we do not find a place, then maybe the building being opened to counteract the sniper with our own sniper getting a shot at him?"

Bill watching them noticed a snarl on Tony's face saying, "my partner, ...Nicola, will be doing that job!" Nicola nodded.

Diane replied, "and I will be her spotter." This time, Tony looked at them and they both nodded.

Bill told Diane to drive to the next village and he would point out the place where the ceremony was to take place.

Tony got on the radio and informed Mike what they had been seen and decided.
Mike replied, "yes, find the buildings he may use and stake out as much as you all can at each building.
You only have today as tomorrow, the Prince arrives, and he will go straight to the ceremony. He will be well protected, but you'll are the only ones who know and can recognise him, so go for it and I want all of you to be armed. The protection people will be told of your presence. Good luck."

So, they went to the area and observed every building a sniper could possibly use including the top of the building the Prince was to open with a plaque and make a short speech.
They introduced themselves and briefed the local police contingent and the Chief Inspector, who assured them that his force was experienced and trained in the protection of high-risk people.
After this, Nicola, Diane, Tony, and Bill, who was now part of their team, decided to have an evening meal at a restaurant that Bill recommended.

They had a nice evening and enjoyed the chance to relax a little.

But all of them knew the next day was to be taxing and nerve racking to the extreme as it mainly depended on them choosing the right building to find Joe in.

The did not stay late and headed back to their hotel knowing they would not get a lot of sleep.

Then morning came, the air was fresh, the sun had risen at 4 am and the sky at was cloudy.
They had their kits ready in the car boot and by 5 am were at the police station in the canteen having a cooked breakfast
The police had already sent their squads out to cover all eventualities. Nicola and Diane had donned their camouflage overalls and by 7am were on the roof of the building for the ceremony. They had their flasks and sandwiches, ready for a long wait.

Tony was with Bill; they were organising the police stake out at the entrance to the buildings they estimated Joe would use.
Bill would stake out those places that he thought would be the ideal place to shoot from.

Tony would tour the crowd and the area to see if he could spot Joe any where!

CHAPTER 27

The Elimination

Joe was up early on the Saturday morning; today was the day he would attempt to assassinate the Arab Prince

He soon had his shower and was tucking into his cooked breakfast.

His mind was focused though on one thing and that was the short drive to the local building where the ceremony to unveil the plaque was taking place.

He put the items he required in his car boot, including his raincoat and anything else he thought he would need. He put the sniper rifle in the false bottom of his case to carry it together with the ammunition required.

He smelt the air which drifted in from the sea, it was mixed with the smell of the pine trees near his cabin. He stopped for a moment to slowly look around the area he was standing in as though he thought he would not see it again.

Shaking his head, he then thought, "why wouldn't I see all this again?" and then he shivered.

He packed his clothes in his case intending to drive off back to London after he had completed the task and escape from the opening ceremony and the assassination.

Joe had the routes that he had to take to the ceremony and the way back to the London Borough where he lived, in his mind.

He wanted to leave the cabin before anyone was out and about. He had disguised himself as an old man with the walking stick. He had used this disguise when he had gone to Hyde Park in London to meet Mack to discuss the assassination contract.

He had everything he required in the car, so he drove off down his path to the big gates, which he opened through a remote control.

He closed the gates after he drove through them with the remote control and then set off on his journey.

When he arrived in the town, he saw police preparations in progress, with barriers and one-way systems which would direct crowds and the Prince to the ceremony.

The sun was out, and it was getting warm.

Joe drove to a road where he could park the car, and which was not too far from the 4-story block of flats he had chosen to fire his shot from.

It was on the top floor in the corner, giving him a clear sight of his target.

He took everything that he needed from the boot of the car and then slowly walked down the road turning right and right again to the entrance of a block of flats.

As he got near the entrance of the flats, he saw a man with a police officer checking everyone who entered and left the building.

They stopped him as he neared the entrance and said, "sorry sir, we have to check bags of everyone going in and out today for security reasons."

Joe held his breath as the police officer undid his case, but luckily seeing a pile of clothes, the officer lifted some and seeing that a few were dirty, he said to Joe, "looks like you need some washing doing!"

Joe smiled and in an older person's voice, he replied, "yes, do you know of anyone?" The policeman laughed and said "go on inside sir and sort yourself out. Sorry we had to stop you."

Joe breathed a sigh of relief, thanked him, walked towards the lifts, and went up to the flat. He opened a window and surveyed the view. He was happy but saw that he would have to move his angle to cut down the glare of the sun.

"Well," he thought to himself, "only an hour to go." So, he poured himself a cup of coffee from the flask he had brought with him and then sat and waited for the appearance of the celebrity.

With the secret service and police in place, Tony and Bill attached themselves to any group they thought had anything to look at or talk to.

Tony spent a lot of his time walking amongst the crowds that had now gathered to see if he could spot Joe or if he could spot anything suspicious.

Once or twice, he stopped a male who looked very similar to Joe, but it was not him.

All the main team of inspectors, etc., had radios that they were asked to use to keep contact on.

Tony decided to move a bit further away from the main ceremony area when he heard a report from a group of two officers who were stopping people before and after they were to going into a building that they thought could be used by a sniper. This report just informed the control that they had stopped and searched an elderly male with a walking stick carrying a case and that he was the only one they had encountered since they had been there!

Tony said into his mike, "can you give me the place the last report came from please? I would like to speak to the person who made it. Over. Tony MI5."

A voice replied, "PC 149, at the grange block of flats, sir. Over."

Tony said, "How many floors? Over"

"Two, to three stories high, sir. Over."

"Get an armed police van there. I'm coming now. One of the eliminator's we know disguises himself as an elderly male. Keep an eye on the window of his flat. I am coming to see if anything like the tip of a gun is near the open window."

Tony set off running; it was no more than two streets away.

On his way, Nicola came on saying, "I have the open window in my sights, get there as quick as you can Tony, it's the only clue we have. I will be training my scope on the window."

Tony came up to a stationary police car, he showed his ID pass and said, "get me to the Grange flats as quick as you can." They did this, without a siren, in 8 minutes.

Tony ran out the car saying to the two guards at the entrance, "follow me" and as he arrived at the door of the flat, he listened and heard a rifle bolt putting a round up. He then thanked the police car driver and told him to inform the armed squad to make their way up to the flat at the end top floor with the widow open.

He and the other two guards went into the building, knocked on the office door and a lady answered. Tony showed his ID pass and explained that he wanted a key to get into the end flat.

The three of them then went up the stairs as fast as they could. He listened, and he could just about hear a rifle bolt being used. So, he unlocked the door took his firearm out, put his shoulder to the door and went in low.

He saw Joe turn and hesitate but before he had a chance to fire a shot, he heard a shot, saw Joe drop the rifle and fall to the floor and a voice in his ear saying, "I got him, he moved into view at the window. Over".

Tony was breathing heavy. The other agent checked to see if Joe was still alive, he was not.

Three armed police arrived after the special agent had called an ambulance and reported Joe's death.

Tony looked out the window that had a good view of the ceremony which had now been completed. The Arab Prince was safe.

Nicola said into the mike, "Tony... Diane and I will come and pick you up. Thank goodness you remembered that Joe liked to disguise as an elderly man. See you in a few minutes. Over."

A police inspector came up to Tony to ask if he was ok. Tony nodded yes and said he would let them have his report, through MI5 or MI6.

He left the room and was in the building's front entrance when Nicola drove up.

She waved, he got in the car and they drove off.

On their way back to London, Tony briefed Mike

on what had happened and said he would write up a full report later using his iPad.

Mike congratulated all of them and said, "take care and have a good journey."

At that moment in time in London, Special Branch arrested Peter Morre on terrorist activities under that Act. He of course had got a top-class lawyer to defend him

Sir Ralph was also held under the Terrorism Act and was being investigated.

Steve was now able to see and talk to Pat. She told him that she had been able to set in motion the forced resignation of Peter, as a director of the company, as her shares and her father's shares were the majority holding. She worked with him to get this pushed through for the good of the firm.

CHAPTER 28

The Aftermath

It was a new year, late spring and Steve had decided after his illness and the lows in his life that it was time to hand over the reins of his business to his partners, Diane, and Tony.

Tony had married Nicola, who had left MI6. She was very happy to run the business from the office and be a housewife. She was also now pregnant with their first child and looking forward to the baby's arrival.

Tony was happy to take on the business of cases, which when compared with the Morre case, they were mostly humdrum and easy going. They were also still employed by Pat to provide bodyguard protection for her company.

Diane was still single and was happy to continue doing investigatory work for the business. She was good at doing this.
They all had their time as witnesses to the crimes of Peter, Joe, and Sir Ralph.

So, life goes on as normal or as normal as they expected.

Steve was now more or less settled in his life. He was still fighting his cancer and knew that his life would never get back to being the same as it was before his diagnosis.
He had gone through 8 weeks of radio therapy, was on injections and a blood test every 6 months. Apart from certain side effects, he now had a near as normal life as was possible.

However, he was getting more tired than ever before and as the weather got warmer and summer was just over the horizon, his thoughts turned to getting a well-earned rest at his favourite area on the east coast near Cromer.

One evening at home, he decided he would go to the place and hotel where he had met Pat and recapture the happy times he had there on his own. He convinced himself it was time to take what pleasures he still could as at this moment in time, he could not plan.
So, the next day he got his PA to book his hotel whilst he made arrangements with his next-door neighbour to look after the garden and his daughter would keep an eye on his home.
He decided he would travel the coming Friday, in two days' time.

He informed everyone at work and even rang Mike, who did not blame him and said, "go and enjoy."

Friday came and the weather turned warmer. He put everything he thought he might need in his car boot, including his pills and then he set off on the A47 to the east coast.

He stopped at the same café as he did the last time and got a shock when he was eating his toast as a similar car to Pat's stopped in the café car park and a nice young lady got out.....but it was not Pat!!
He smiled to himself, shook his head and left soon afterwards to continue his journey.

As he drove along, he heard on the news that the R&H group had merged with the firm who also did MOD contracts and a new shareholding was in the process.
Steve smiled to himself and thought "good for you Pat, you have done it and produced a very large group, your father will be proud of you."

He decided to use the coast road to the Cromer area and passed by the Lavender Fields and the Sandringham estate. He drove slowly enjoying his drive with the smell of the sea, the various stopping places to see docks and fishing boats and the seaside places he had visited from the past.

Eventually by mid-afternoon, he reached his hotel.

He was only in his room for ten minutes before he went down the slope to the beach

The sun was warm, the sky was a deep blue, the sea breeze was nice and smelt of salt water.

He sat under an umbrella on a sun lounger drinking a gin and tonic and was typing on his iPad, at peace with the world. He was completely lost in concentrating on his typing.

Many miles away near the Afghanistan border, a private aircraft was flying very close to the border putting itself in a position of being fired at. It did not have permission from the airspace they were encroaching on to fly there.

The passengers were Bill Wilde and his entourage. They had been on a visit to promote Bill's organisation, SOOWN.

Bill had instructed the pilot to fly close to Afghanistan's air space and this had triggered off two British jet fighter planes to warn them to keep within international air space, as they were putting themselves at risk of being shot at from ground missiles in that area.

The RAF planes caught up with Bill's plane and tried to make radio contact. They did not answer so one of the fast jet's went to the front of Bill's private plane where he could see the pilot. He gave him a hand signal indicating for him to move away and land. The pilot acknowledged with a bad salute.

One RAF pilot then suddenly warned the other pilot to pull back as he had received notification that a ground missile was on its way.
They both sent out anti missile covers and pulled away fast reporting to their control base, their actions. The pilots looked back and saw that the missile had hit the private plane which went down in pieces and hit international soil and rocks.
The RAF planes flew back to base.

Tony rang Steve on his mobile and asked if he had heard the news about an aircraft that had been shot down near Afghanistan's air space. He told him that one of the passengers was Bill Wilde of the SOOWN organisation.
Steve replied, "Couldn't happen to a better person, hey?"
"Yes, strange that they were so close to the border. I suppose someone else will take it over, there is plenty of that type in the world. I don't suppose too many people will be sorry."
Tony laughed and said, "How's the relaxing going?" "Great," replied Steve.

After the call, he put his iPad down and yawned. He got his binoculars out and surveyed the beach and sea. A nice yacht was in full sail and the beach had lots of children enjoying themselves

Steve put his iPad away in his bag and was just about to get up when a female voice said very softly behind him.

"Fancy seeing you here?"

He turned and was amazed to see Pat Morre standing there looking beautiful and cool.

He stood up and gave her a big hug and a long kiss.

In her usual way, she looked at him and said, "I guess you are pleased to see me. I did wonder what reception I would get as I've been so busy. I admit I have not been in touch for a while."

He smiled and replied, "well I have not made a big effort either to keep in touch so let's just be thankful we are together now, as I cannot think of anyone else I would wish to be here."

She grinned, saying, "does that mean you would like me to stay?" He looked at her in the eyes and said nothing, except to kiss her passionately. He then said, "Does that answer your question?"

She looked into his eyes and nodded yes.

He gestured to the waiter to come over, ordered two gin and tonics and then they sat holding hands, talking.

Pat suddenly said to Steve, "I saw you working on your iPad. I hope that was not work?" He laughed and replied, "No, I decided on the way here that the adventure we have had since we met would make a good book, so I have started to write it." She laughingly replied, "So what name have you given me?" He chuckled, saying, "I'm afraid you will have to read the book when it's finished, as we both know it's fiction" and looking at her he continued, "isn't it?"

THE END

Printed in Great Britain
by Amazon

62433515R00149